ONE LADY, TWO CATS

By Richard Lockridge

ONE LADY, TWO CATS

≈≈≈

Richard Lockridge

≈≈≈

J. B. Lippincott Company
PHILADELPHIA AND NEW YORK

For Hildy

Who wrote so much of it

Contents

ONE LADY, TWO CATS

I

Meeting

BEFORE I WENT SOUTH that winter I had, in passing, mentioned cats. I do this with little provocation and it often takes me considerable time to pass a given cat. But in those hurrying weeks I did not talk much of cats, nor in any sense make an issue of them. Other issues were more immediate and became so increasingly as the day I was to leave came closer.

We talked a good deal about my going south; we agreed that it was still a good idea for me to keep an appointment I had made with myself when one appointment seemed as good as any other—had made long before we met. It would, we told each other with assurance which diminished day by day, be a good thing for both of us. It would give us time to think things over, quietly. This was, of course, entire nonsense, but neither of us was then sure enough to state so obvious a fact. So I waited in the ruins of Pennsylvania Station on a morning which was singularly cold and damp until gates opened.

It was warm that winter in Key West, where it is

almost always warm. I had a motel room with sliding glass panels which could be opened on a swimming pool, and a desk almost the right height for a typewriter even if only a portable. I like a solid, phlegmatic typewriter which doesn't mind being hit in the face, and will keep its feet under it. But this was a more pleasant place to work than a Manhattan hotel room had been. It seemed a long way from everywhere, but it was a comfortable place, and one I had known before. I worked on a novel set in Key West, which had been the main reason for going there. With considerably more enthusiasm, I wrote letters. And peered hungrily into the pigeonholes behind the desk clerk, looking for answers from a lady.

A good many letters went from Key West to West Ninth Street that February into March. In one of the first letters I told her that the temperature was around eighty and white clouds were drifting in a bright blue sky above a blue-green ocean—and that I wished I were walking through the rain on Ninth Street, to her apartment.

And in another letter I told her she did not have to like cats. A man in love will make the most unlikely promises. I do not remember that I underlined the word *have*, except perhaps by implication. Her answer, it seemed to me, had in it an element of surprise, even of bewilderment.

It was a matter to which she'd never given much

thought. She did not feel one way or the other about cats. It had been her custom to nod courteously when introduced to the cats of friends, and she expected as much from cats. Beyond that, it was clear, she couldn't care less.

My mentioning weather was different. She had got my letter about the blueness of Key West skies on one of the dreariest, wettest days that winter, when she was in bed with a sinus infection. "But when I went to the doctor to have my sinuses poked, I carried your last three letters along and read them seven times each in the waiting room." She had never known it was humanly possible—or inhumanly possible—to miss somebody so much, she said. She wasn't able to concentrate on her work and that made her pretty indignant. And cheered me. Because earlier she had told me, briskly, "We're both professionals, so we can put everything else out of our minds during working hours." She had bragged, too, about how she always slept nine hours, and distrusted the phrase *slept like a baby* because from the little she'd seen of babies, they kept waking up yelling. And now she was in that state herself, even if she didn't wake up yelling—out loud. "I get up in the night and walk the floor with myself and I'm even reduced to reading poetry instead of mysteries." Did I know the poem of Cummings that ended, "We're wonderful one times one"? And she had thought up two brand-new, subsidiary reasons why she shouldn't marry: she would cost me money because she wouldn't be able to go off on magazine assignments, and she had had to cancel her dental appointments for gum care. "So I will lose all my teeth and you wouldn't want to be married to a toothless crone anyway."

I tackled the money problem first, in my next letter: "This financial burden—I'm interested how you arrived at a figure of sixteen hundred eighty-seven dollars and apparently no cents. Dear child, to be crass about it, you'd save me at least that much on income tax, if we were married. If I continue to make enough to live on. Of which there is no certainty whatever, particularly now when I've been diverted from the comparative safety of mysteries to this strange new novel land. And because of that, and because of you, I'm a strange new man to myself. We may well go broke together. That part of life has always been chancy for me; I see no reason to expect a change. If you lose your teeth—the theory that marrying me would have that result rather baffles me—I don't knock out teeth, I'm a rib crusher—but if you lose your teeth we'll buy you all the new ones you want. Not all of mine are home-grown. And now will you stop loving me? Because of this confession?"

She apologized, by special delivery, "for having, at my advanced age, a girlish, ladies-magazine delusion that love depends on externals." It was a very

1 4

bracing letter, the gist being that she loved the pilgrim soul in me, as well as five or six other sterling qualities; she also liked my looks. She just didn't want to get married.

At cocktail time that same day, when I was sitting in the motel lounge waiting for friends to pick me up, I got a telegram:

WHAT COLOR ARE YOUR EYES? HOW COULD I HAVE KNOWN YOU TEN WEEKS TWO DAYS AND STILL BE IGNORANT ON THIS VITAL POINT? WHY HAVE YOU KEPT ME IN THE DARK? MUST KNOW AT ONCE. URGENT.

I had thought of my eyes, vaguely, as greenish. But my friends the Frasches, who drove up just then, had a different opinion. Several different opinions. They took me off to their house and over Martinis they debated the question with spirit. Charles thought my eyes were more "grayish-yellow" than greenish. Martha said *hazel;* when Martha comes to a decision, she comes to it with something like violence. "Tell her positively hazel. No *ish* about it. Phone her right now."

They shut me, tactfully, into a bedroom, and I phoned a New York number I knew better than my own, and told Hildy my eyes were hazel. Since it had taken several Martinis to settle this, I may have sounded a bit free-floating: "And yours are Siamese blue," I said. "Did I ever yowl like a cat for you?" It's quite a good yowl—it has brought cats running—and I gave it my best delivery on the phone. "You sound like a tomcat," Hildy said.

I assured her, at costly length, that I was a domestic, hearthside sort. And I wrote her later: "I wouldn't insist on marriage on moral grounds. But it's more convenient when two people want to register at a motel. . . . I don't intend to let you and your sinus spend another winter in New York. Not if I have anything to say about it—and I will. You keep saying you feel 'much better.' How long can you keep getting better without getting well?"

She promised to be well by the time I got back—and yes, she would love to go up with me to my house in the country and meet my cats.

I don't remember that we mentioned cats again, on the phone or in letters.

And cats were not at all on my mind when I walked again through what remained of Penn Station, expecting workmen who were destroying it to fall from scaffolding onto my head. I was on the last car of a long train and so farthest from the dank passage which led into a dank afternoon. I had trouble finding a redcap. Most of the other passengers reached the taxi ramp, which taxi drivers were assiduously avoiding, long before I did.

Hildy was walking back and forth at the end of

the passageway, stopping now and then to peer into it. She has a quick, gay way of walking. It was a fine afternoon . . .

A day or two later, Helen drove my ancient Buick in from the country and stopped at the hotel for me, and we drove west through Ninth Street to the apartment. Hildy was waiting for us in the lobby, with her bag. I was pleased to see that it was definitely bigger than overnight size, bigger even than weekend. I said their names to them, "Mrs. Holmes—Miss Dolson," and watched them meet. I had no doubts about their meeting.

As Hildy remembers it, I had written her, after assuring her that she did not have to like cats, that she did have to like Helen. If I wrote that, I fumbled words. Liking Helen does not require compulsion.

I had told her about Helen, of course—how for a good many years she had kept house for two people, and how, for more than two years, she had cared for one person when he was listless in the house. And I had written Helen after I moved to New York the previous November, not expecting to find anything in New York either, that I had met a Miss Hildegarde Dolson at a cocktail party and had been seeing a good bit of her. When I wrote Helen from Key West I may have gone further, but I could not have been explicit because then I had nothing certain to tell her. I do not think I told her that one of the magazine pieces

Miss Dolson had written long before we met was titled, "Why I'd Make an Awful Wife."

Probably I was not really at all subtle about it; certainly Helen has got to know me well through the years and become sensitive to the inflections of my voice and perceptive about the words I use, even on paper. She is one of the most perceptive people I've ever known. When she and Hildy shook hands, it seemed to me that both women were reacting with more than good-manners pleasantness. They were *pleased.*

I put Hildy in the front seat beside me, and drove the ten-year-old Buick through a tangle of traffic to the West Side Highway, and turned up it. I fitted the car into a lane.

Then, over my shoulder, I asked Helen how the cats were; whether the driveway had fallen in, as it usually does in the spring, and whether many people had been around to look at the house. I put my questions in the order of importance, and Helen took them that way. If Hildy was surprised by the sequence—she knew I had been trying to sell the house for upwards of a year—she did not show it.

The cats were fine, Helen said. On good days they were going out of doors again. The deworming which had been necessary during the winter seemed to have been a success. I asked interested questions; Helen went into details. Hildy suddenly rolled down

her window and it occurred to me that the deworming of cats was a subject she might not be used to,
before lunch. Helen said quickly that Sherry was putting on weight now. And Pammy was interested in,
but did not seem to be very hopeful about, the birds
which gathered under the feeders.

I didn't think birds, in that context, were any
safer than worms; the driveway was solider. Helen
said it had taken early spring with unusual firmness.
We would have no real trouble getting in. The oil
truck had made it recently—made it in and, with no
great difficulty, out again. This last was encouraging;
during the time it takes to pump oil out of a truck
into a tank the truck has a tendency to sink.

As to prospects—yes, there had been a few. Earlier in the week there had been a couple who had
seemed quite interested. The woman had come first,
and then, the next day, come back with her husband
and, of course, the real-estate agent.

Unfortunately, Helen told us, she had just waxed
the living-room floor. She had been sorry; she couldn't
let them in. They would have tracked everything up.
There had been some talk of spreading newspapers
on the floor, but this had not seemed to Helen a good
idea. And there had also been, of course, the problem
of the big black ants.

Every three or four years, black ants arrive with
the spring, and arrive in force. They are nothing time

and ant traps will not cope with; they are rather un-
sightly but do no damage I have ever noticed. The
cats do not eat them, although they are rather fond of
most insects. Ants are pretty acid.

"You told the prospects about the ants?" I asked
Helen, and she said she had. And that, anyway, the
prospects had only to look around them. Black ants
on a green tile floor are highly visible.

Helen hoped she hadn't made a mistake. The
prospects would really have tracked up the floor and
she hadn't wanted Miss Dolson to see it first with
mud all over it. The real-estate agent had been quite
put out and Helen was sorry about that, but there
hadn't seemed to be anything else to do. And she
couldn't very well deny the ants.

I told her she had done fine; that she had done
just right.

"I thought you might feel that way," Helen said,
with no special inflection. It wasn't until much later
that she told me, "If I'd thought there was any real
danger of this house being sold before you brought
Miss Dolson up, I'd have bred more black ants."

It was still like winter that day we first drove toward northern Westchester and a house fifty-odd
miles from New York. Near the city there was, for a
little distance, that just discernible haze on some of
the trees which shows that they have begun to bud
toward the spring. There was no color in the haze, as

in a few weeks there would be. Farther up the Saw
Mill River Parkway it was all winter still and the trees
were bare. Where evergreens or stone fences had
given shade, the snow held on. When I took the familiar, always shaded, bypass road at the end of the
Saw Mill, Helen said it had been iced over when she
drove in. It wasn't, that late morning, except in a few
patches.

"It's pretty country in the spring and summer,"
I told Hildy, reassuring a city woman who had spent
the longer part of her life in New York. "It's rolling
country. The house is on a ridge."

I knew she'd grown up in a small town in western
Pennsylvania, and had written a book about her decidedly non-city childhood. I had read the book and
delighted in it. But that morning in the last week of
March, I kept telling her, as if she'd never seen grass
or trees before, that this bleak wilderness would soon
be bursting green.

As we made the last turn toward the house I
stopped talking and devoted myself to worrying.
Helen had got down the drive all right, but it is easier
to get down it—if you haven't sunk in the turnaround
—than to get up it. The house, I realized, would show
its need of paint. I had not painted it the summer
before because people who bought it would want to
choose their own new color. And there was always
the matter of the cats. Hildy might merely have been

polite when she said she had, so far as she knew, no rooted objection to cats.

The drive was all right—rutted, of course, but passable. We slithered only slightly as we turned up the incline from the road and into the curve which follows. I'd known it worse. In the slanting spring sunlight the house did show need of paint. But the old paint was not actually scaled off.

The cats had heard the car and knew the car. They sat side by side behind the front-door glass and looked at the car. They appeared darker than I remembered them. That had always been true; returning after even a few weeks away I had always been mildly surprised by how dark my cats were. Sitting behind the glass that afternoon, with not much more than faces and ears showing, they looked very dark indeed. Being seal-point Siamese there was obviously nothing they could do about it. I managed to avoid telling Hildy that, when we were closer, she would see that they really sparkled and that their eyes were very blue.

We got out of the car, hauling suitcases out of it, and of course the cats ran. Sherry ran to the landing at the top of the stairs, where she would be nearest an open door and the refuge to be found under a bed. Pammy went only halfway up and stopped to watch. All this was to be expected.

All cats I have ever known have taken a dim view

of luggage. Suitcases mean one of two things to them: either people they know and trust are going away, and deserting cats, or strangers are invading the cats' house. There is also, I suppose, the knowledge that suitcases are awkward things and may bump into cats.

But Pammy, that day, stood her step—more precisely, crouched her step. She waited until the door was open and Hildy had gone into the house. As Hildy went in, her heels tapped on the tile floor. Pammy listened to that and looked down, for some seconds, at a quick, slight woman she had never seen before. Then she went to join Sherry under a bed.

"Well," I said, "this is it." I have, I hope, made brighter remarks. We put bags down in the entrance hall. Helen, although she could not have known how Hildy is about flowers, had filled a vase with daffodils from a greenhouse. There were no muddy tracks on the polished floor, at least until the three of us went into it. Sunlight splashed through bright windows onto green tile. Sunlight also, rather too brightly, lighted fabrics cats had tattered. The cats had had a busy winter.

"It's a lovely big room," Hildy said, and did not say anything about the shredded upholstery—did not even look at it with obvious intentness. "That's the most beautiful fireplace I've ever seen." And she told Helen how nice it was to come into a room with yellow flowers in it, because yellow was her favorite color.

We took her suitcase to the upstairs guest room, where sun was strong as a searchlight. The green walls looked a bit spotty to me; two drawings of kittens which had been put up to cover the worst-faded spots were on the wall facing the twin beds. I was relieved to see that the fresh white bedspreads were free of paw marks, and no depressions in the pillows, which meant the cats hadn't napped there.

I showed Hildy where things were, and found out that sherry on the rocks would be a suitable pre-lunch drink. I had made it clear that one thing I would never do for her was to drink sherry myself. "Any more than I'd drink a Martini," Hildy said. Amiably, but with a firmness that may have come down from her paternal Dutch ancestors. She's Scotch-Irish on the other side, which is a good thing.

I went down to fix us drinks while Helen got our lunch. And for the first time I heard the quick clicking of heels as Hildy walked on bare oak flooring through the short corridor from guest bedroom to guest bath.

I dropped ice into a short glass and into a cocktail mixer and waited for heels to click again and thought that for a long time the house had been silent. This was not really true; houses which live by electricity talk of it. Furnaces go on and refrigerators

click into life and hum up the cold; there are unex-
plained cracklings as the temperature changes. Lights
dim momentarily and ears wait for the um—*uh!* um—
uh! of the water pump. It is not really a silent house.
And it is one built for resonance. It had long been a
silent house.

Heels clicked again and I poured sherry on ice in
the small glass, and gin and vermouth into the mixer.
As I turned away from the bar with the glasses, I
looked up the room and into the sunlight. The cats
had really gone to work on chairs and sofas. A sofa by
the television cabinet had an arm ripped to shreds;
stuffing dribbled out. Two other chairs were patched.
It was expert patching; Helen had long fought with
tireless skill against the tatters. Cats are tireless too:
the sofas at right angles nearest the dining room were
ripped across the bottoms, so that threads dangled. It
will look awful to Hildy, I thought, remembering her
attractive, well-ordered apartment where nothing was
torn. It will give her a bad impression of my cats. It
will give her something to have against them.

Her heels tapped down the stairs and, with a different pitch, on the tiles of the living-room floor. She
sat beside me on a sofa and we clicked glasses and
she said it was a fine house, a house with good, clear
space. She still didn't seem to see the torn fabrics, but
she did stare in a baffled way at one object placed
prominently near a lamp table. "What's that pedestal

thing wrapped in a cloth?" I said it was a scratching post. "The idea is that cats claw it instead of furniture."

"Oh," she said, tactfully not pointing out that the idea didn't seem to have worked. "Where are they now? Are they boycotting me?"

I said it was the luggage more than anything else. And one of them—the one named Sherry—was afraid of almost everything that walked on two legs. I started to tell Hildy why, but thought of better things to say to her. We drank slowly, talking of other things than cats. The furnace cleared its throat in the startled way it has and coughed slightly and settled to its job. And a small thumping started on the staircase.

Pammy. I said, "You can always tell—she has to come down one step at a time because she's shorter and cobbier."

"It looks just like the other one to me," Hildy said.

"Don't call a cat 'it,'" I said. "You may call babies 'it'—I always do, myself—but you may not call a cat 'it.' Not in my presence."

"Yes, dear," the lady said. In the tone one uses to humor small cretins.

Pammy hopped from last step to floor and went to look out the front door to see, again, what kind of day it was. We looked at her, with the sun on her sleek coat, which was, in shadings, the color of coffee laced with cream, set off by the black-coffee markings. She had not looked at us, although she was entirely conscious of us. I said, "Hello, Pammy," across the room, and the utmost tip of her long brown tail twitched. She did not turn toward us. She turned her head a little and looked at the gnarled apple tree. A bluejay flashed into the apple tree and Pammy, without special animus, swished her tail at it. Then she looked another way, since there might be something of special interest in the garage. But there was nothing which required an additional swish of a long brown tail.

Hildy said, "Hi, Pammy." No answer. Not even a nod.

"This will teach you not to bring strange ladies home with you. She is snubbing me."

"I'm the one being snubbed," I said. "She's punishing me because I went away for a long time and left her. And cats are more reserved than dogs, anyway."

"When people heard I was coming up to visit you, they kept asking me, 'But do you love cats?' Some of them sounded as if I ought to put catnip behind my ears like perfume."

"My cats are bored by catnip," I said.

The second sound of the word "cat" did it, as I had thought it might. The tip of Pammy's tail twitched again. Then she turned to look at us. She did not turn her body. She turned her head and looked back over her shoulder. One puts human thoughts into feline minds, where they have no place. She seemed to regard us with surprise. She looked at us for some seconds. Then she turned to face us and stretched, long and slow, her tail curving up along her back. Then she sat down facing us and fully looked at us.

It was bright in the room that afternoon in very early spring. Because it was bright the pupils of Pammy's eyes were slits and the irises round and blue, startling against the dark mask of her face. She wrapped her tail around her and studied us across the room with that unblinking gaze of the cat—the gaze which always makes me wonder, a little uneasily, what it is cats really see.

She had her back to the door and the sunlight fell again on her shining coat. She is in good condition, I thought, without quite thinking. No spikiness. She's a little more cross-eyed than I remember her. But when I come back, she always is.

"She has a charming face," Hildy said, sounding rather surprised.

"Actually, it's too round for her breed. They want them pointed now. 'Wedge-shaped,' they call it." I was making noises, as lady looked at cat and cat at lady—blue-eyed lady at blue-eyed cat. I thought, with pleasure, it's probably the first time she's ever studied a cat.

"Weasels are pointy," Hildy said. "The breeders are crazy if they make Siamese ferretish for a fad."

At the second hearing—really hearing—of a voice she did not know, Pammy moved both her brown, pointed ears forward, concentrating on this new sound. She did not otherwise move, but sat and looked at us down the length of a long room. I thought, She's a beauty. Even if she is several pounds overweight. She has the sweetest, gayest. . . . Aloud I said modestly, "Of course she'd never be accepted for show."

"You wouldn't put a cat in a *show*," Hildy said. "Like renting your child out to be a movie star. Or for TV commercials, lisping. Pammy wouldn't be caught dead in a show. Would you, Pammy?"

Pammy did not say anything. But the tip of her tail moved up from the floor and down again and then up again and down again.

She got up and stretched once more, which I thought a little ostentatious of her. Then she went off, at her own pace, which was not rapid, around the foot of the staircase and into a hallway which leads to the kitchen. Helen was in the kitchen, and it was almost time for Pammy's lunch and, for that matter, ours. I heard the soft thud which meant that Pammy had leaped up to the counter where her food might be and the slightly heavier thump as she dropped down to the floor again, having discovered that lunch was not yet served.

There are two ways into and out of the kitchen. The one Pammy took leads around the center chimney, on the far side of the big brick fireplace. The other is by way of a door which opens, which swings when it is not on check, between kitchen and living room.

It was open that day while Helen waited for the signal eye of the waffle iron to redden. Pammy came and sat in the doorway and looked at us again, much as she had before; as unblinkingly as she had before.

"Come over here and meet the lady," I said.

Pammy did answer this time. She was never one to raise her voice, and she did not raise it then. Siamese cats seldom say "miaou" in any of its imitative spellings. Pammy said the Siamese equivalent of "Yanh" softly. Then she trotted over to the nearest patched chair, stood up on her hind legs, dug her front claws deep into fabric, and gave a loud r-r-r-rip.

"Stop it," I said.

Pammy clawed again. And again. And again.

"*Pammy!*" I shouted. "*Stop it! Right now.*"

Pammy flexed her claws and went on ripping.

"It's just one of the things you have to expect," I said. "If you're going to keep cats."

Hildy was eloquently silent.

"This is mild, compared to some of them. My friends the Haycrafts had a long-hair who ripped off big pieces of wallpaper. Expensive new decorator wallpaper."

Hildy ground out her cigarette in an ash tray decorated with kittens, one of those weekend presents bestowed on the Lockridge household because of the cat motif.

"And I've known cats that raced up and down curtains and clawed them to ribbons," I said. "And once, when a friend gave a party, his cat ate a big chunk out of a guest's cashmere coat left on a bed."

Pammy, tired of ripping for the moment, squatted down near the fireplace and began to wash her rear end. To anyone unaccustomed to cats, it's a somewhat unusual position.

Hildy began to laugh rather hysterically.

Pammy's head came up sharply, questioningly.

"She's not laughing at you, Pammy," I said.

The lady said, "No, Pammy, I'm not laughing at you." But then she said, "Darling." And she wasn't looking at my cat.

II

Approach

WE SAT UP rather late that night, looking at the fire.
Without cats. They had gone upstairs to the big bedroom which was always theirs until humans wanted it
to sleep in.

The staircase from the entrance hall leads up to a
landing, and to a door that opens on a corridor con-
necting the big bedroom and its bath and the room
I work in. From the landing, a balcony reaches to the
front of the house and the guest-room door.

Hildy went up first, and I called after her to be
sure the latch on her door caught, as it did not always.
A door, particularly one on which the latch does not
always fully engage, is a challenge to any cat. At the
least, such a door will rattle. If paws push hard
enough, it will sometimes open. I heard her door close
firmly and afterward the quick tapping of her heels.
I turned out lights and locked doors and drew the
screen across the fireplace opening.

It had been a good many months since the cats'
possession of the big bedroom had been challenged,

Sherry was another matter. She was not under the bed, but that still left quite a choice of hiding places. The bedroom is directly over the living room, and almost as big, with a fireplace. There is an upholstered chair with scant clearance from the floor and so not often her first choice. She was not under it, either. There was, for some minutes, nothing to do but wait. I didn't want to rush the game, because I'd neglected cats ever since I came home, for good reason. Pammy had forgiven me. Now I hoped to make my peace with Sherry, if I let her set the pace. But I was down to my shorts and shivering with cold, before one of the curtains which reach to the floor behind the sofa moved slightly. It was then only necessary to move the sofa and shake the curtains. There was, of course, always a good chance she would come out and hide under the bed. That night she did not: she streaked for corridor and open door. She had learned early, tragically, not to trust humans, and for the moment I was back in that vast horde of untrustables. And I was too tired to do anything about it right then.

When I went to close the hall door after her, I saw there was still light showing under the guest-room door . . .

Cats can sleep in most lights, sometimes with a forepaw shielding eyes like a mask. But morning light almost always wakens them. Dawn came early that and I thought, momentarily, they might have forgotten. They had not. When I went into the room, leaving the hall door open behind me, the bedroom was empty of cats. I closed the office door and the bathroom door so that cats, when the game was over, would have but one exit.

Pammy had gone under the bed, which was to be expected. She had, however, left her tail sticking out, which was only to be hoped for. One of my cats, who was named Martini, had been most particular about her tail. It was not to be touched by anybody; when she had kittens she would not let them play with her own and very special tail. Pammy accepted her tail more casually, regarding it as merely another part of cat. She did not appear much to mind its being used as a handle.

I made, that first night of my return, noises which were supposed to indicate that I was preoccupied with other things—which certainly was true enough— and so indifferent to the presence of cats. I tried to drift, as if by chance, into reach of the forgotten tail. I crouched suddenly and grabbed and my luck held. Pammy held too—held with claws set in rug under the bed. But she did not make any special to-do about it, and, when I prized her out and held her, she purred in my arms. When I scratched softly behind her pointed ears she snuggled against me. I carried her to the landing and she bumped downstairs.

APPROACH

morning and so did cats, and their methods had not
changed. They came to the landing and bumped
frenziedly. They hurled each other against the door,
producing fine banging sounds. I woke slowly, with a
feeling of insufficient sleep. (Which was true enough;
I had not gone to sleep quickly, for one reason and
another.) Let the cats—I woke fully, and realized
that I could not let the cats. Hildy had long lived
alone; called herself "a loner"; had set her hours of
living and of working. Early rising was not included
in her habits; one did not telephone her, in the mornings, before eleven. The house is resonant. In a moment, Sherry would ——

I got out of bed much more abruptly than is my
custom, but I was not abrupt enough. Or perhaps I
was not quiet enough. Sherry heard my movement
and Sherry began to talk about it—about the closed
door, the hunger of cats, the unacceptable sluggish-
ness of humans.

There is no adequate way of describing Sherry's
voice when she decides to speak up. She is Siamese,
and Siamese cats do not speak as other cats. The pitch
is very different. And Sherry, as an individual, has a
voice of, sometimes, almost unbearable penetration.
She produces tones which must, I think, surprise even
her. Now and then, in the middle of a yowl, she seems
to hear herself and stops abruptly in what I take to
be astonishment. Or perhaps it is pride.

In those days she spoke for both cats when it was time to waken humans. This was, I always assumed, by prearrangement. Certainly they seemed to arrange a good many things between themselves, sometimes after no little conversation. Their words, if they used words, were beyond human comprehension. A good many humans, talking or writing of their cats, substitute human for feline speech and this has never seemed to me useful. Cats do not talk English and this may be especially true of Siamese cats. So I do not contend that, those mornings on the landing, Pammy actually said to Sherry, "All right, friend. Let them have it."

I was standing on one foot that morning, putting the other into slacks, when Sherry let me have it. She had, I thought while I struggled to regain balance, been saving up for months. She said "Yow-*ow!* Yah-*ow*" and all the usual things and ended with a shriek which entirely defies transliteration. She emits it now and then when, in the course of a lengthy announcement, she finds it necessary to yawn.

"I'm coming, for God's sake," I said, keeping my own voice as low as I could while getting intensity into it. "I'm *coming.*"

That was a mistake. Spoken to, Sherry answers. She answered my assurance, and from the tone she used, she rejected it utterly. She also, if one could judge by sounds, backed off a few feet and hurled herself at the door. The thud was an impressive thud.

They would wake Hildy up. Probably they had already. Of course they had already. I looked at my watch as I strapped it on. At eight-thirty. Which was not, clearly, going to enhance her appreciation of cats or of those who harbored cats. The ugly possibility that she would not only get up but pack up snaggled in my mind. On awakening I am always a little inclined to anticipate disaster.

I got the door open. The two cats sat side by side on the landing. They looked up at me from the most innocent of blue eyes. Then they led me down the stairs in their usual fashion—Sherry ran down, a streak of cat; Pammy went from step to step, stopping on each tread and always at the spot where I had planned to put a foot. It took Pammy and me a little while to reach the kitchen, where Sherry was waiting —and wailing of starvation.

Pammy floated up to her counter and eagerly impeded my efforts to open a jar of junior beef and divide it between two metal pans. Sherry sat on the floor and wailed. Pammy began to eat at once, and Sherry screamed at us both. I put Sherry's food on the floor. She sniffed it contemptuously. Then she went to the kitchen door and yelled at it. I let her out. Pammy looked over her shoulder. When I closed the door, Pammy dropped lightly to the floor to eat Sherry's breakfast while the chance offered.

Nothing had changed very much. Nothing, in fact, had changed at all.

I put the coffee water on and squeezed juice from oranges. And heels clicked along the hallway overhead. Resentfully? But she did not walk as if she were carrying anything heavy, such as a suitcase. Probably she would wait to pack until she had had coffee. I got butter out of the refrigerator to soften up for toast. I got out eggs and remembered I had forgotten to ask Hildy whether she would want eggs for breakfast. I poured boiling water over the coffee in the filter cone and went into the living room and lighted a cigarette, which is something I try to avoid doing until after a swallow of coffee. I can so assure myself that I do not smoke before breakfast. The point didn't, that morning, seem worth making.

The guest-room door opened and closed again and heels tapped quickly along the balcony. I could see Pammy in the kitchen, still eating Sherry's breakfast. Pammy looked up and back toward the sound and sat for a moment crouched, her head turned. But then she went back to eating and the heels tapped on the stairs.

Hildy was not carrying a suitcase and she was not dressed for going anywhere. She had on a long yellow robe and mules. When I stood up she said, "Hi," in what seemed a most cheerful manner. She did not look as if she had slept badly and when I asked her about it she said she had slept very well; better than she usually did in a strange place. I said, "I was afraid the cats ——"

"They bounced up and down a bit," she said. "Around three A.M. I thought they might be playing leapfrog."

A blanket chest is on the balcony opposite the guest-room door. There are usually plants on it in the winter and early spring, but there is still room for cats and, sitting on the chest, a cat can look out a window. They do thump, of course, when they land on it, and when they land on the floor again. But I had a feeling they'd stepped up the act last night.

Hildy did not want eggs for breakfast—juice and coffee and a piece of toast. I went to the kitchen for them, and for coffee for myself. Pammy had gone back to her counter to see if her own breakfast had a better taste than Sherry's. She dropped off it when I was pouring coffee from Chemex to pot and went to the back door, then looked back at the lady. I opened the door fast, but she took her time about going, having to taste the air and look from side to side and look up to see that nothing threatened. I nudged her gently with a foot and she went out.

"One of them knocked at my door," Hildy said. "Just before I turned off the light. It sounded as if a person was knocking. I thought you wanted to tell me something, but when I called your name, a cat answered."

"There was a guest once who heard a knock and leaped up and opened the door. She was surprised when a cat walked in and went under the bed. I'm sorry they bothered you. I could keep them shut up in the kitchen at night."

There was an assumption in what I said and for a moment I wished I hadn't said it. But all Hildy said was, "They wouldn't like to be shut up," and that I made good coffee and did I know whether Helen had any unflavored gelatin in the house—she always put it in her orange juice. I didn't know. I said Helen would be ordering when she came in and that I'd ask her to put gelatin on the list. Hildy didn't say I shouldn't.

She did ask where "they" were now and I said they had gone out; that, when weather permitted as it did today, they were outdoor cats and liked to hunt. That was a mistake. Hildy's eyebrows wiggled upward and I waited gloomily for the question.

"Birds?"

I poured more coffee and lighted a cigarette. Hildy is not a woman to be sidetracked; she gives off vibrations.

"Not too often," I said. "They've been around quite a while. And learned, as most grown cats learn, that there's easier hunting to be had." I said birds sometimes even attack cats. I mentioned the great horned owl; I described the horrors of a poor helpless cat caught in those giant claws and devoured. Admittedly, there aren't too many great horned owls in Westchester County. I told about one cat of mine who was set upon by a flight of swallows which circled above her, peeling off one by one, and in evidently planned sequence, to dive-bomb her. However she leaped, the attacking swallow was always just beyond reach, and in the end my cat cowered against a terrace door, crying for rescue.

There is no doubt that I often talk of cats.

"My family ran to dogs," Hildy said. "Airedales mostly. We preferred big dogs."

I was prepared to offer dog stories too. I told Hildy about our long-time vet in New York, Dr. Camuti, and the time he tangled with a dog. "Camuti is one of the greatest cat vets in the country, but this happened when he was a young man just starting in practice. He got a call to come up to the Bronx and 'put away' a dog. Camuti put on his one good suit, a brown wool. And he bought chloroform to finish off the dog painlessly. He rode uptown thinking of the cash fee he'd collect when he'd put a poor old wheezing pet out of its misery.

"When the woman let Camuti into the apartment, a Great Dane the size of a horse bounded out and nearly knocked him flat. That was the 'poor old wheezing pet'—leaping all over the place. The woman said the dog had belonged to her late husband and she didn't want to give him to strangers, but he was just too big for an apartment.

"Dr. Camuti had been reluctant from the start; a veterinarian's purpose is to save, not to destroy—not to 'put to sleep.' The Dane looked anything but sleepy. But Camuti had promised, and he is a resolute man. He got Dane and chloroform into a bathroom. He opened the bottle and the dog lunged at him playfully . . .

"Dr. Camuti was very wet, because a woman was pouring water on him. From the floor he looked up into the face of a Great Dane, who was evidently laughing. Camuti did not laugh back. When he was able he got off the bathroom floor and out of the apartment, swaying somewhat as he walked. But when the woman asked him if he would be back, there was no wavering in his voice. 'No,' Dr. Camuti said. His wet suit shrank rapidly on the subway going home, a ride which, he had told me those years after, took his last five cents. He never did get reimbursed for the chloroform."

When Camuti treated my cats, many years later, he had considerably more cents than I had. I told Hildy how he would ring the doorbell of our Village apartment in a special way the cats recognized, and how they'd run and hide. "We'd spend a half hour finding cats, then Camuti would treat the sick one in ten minutes, and spend another hour over coffee, telling me stories."

Hildy said, "Tell me some more."

I told her more. And I told her about a dog who is now a legend in Ridgefield: Gretchen of the Elms Inn. "Gretchen was so huge that every time she came into the bar and sat down, the ancient timbers would quake. One day she was hurrying across Main Street and bumped into a Packard so hard she crumpled the fender. Gretchen herself wasn't dented." I said I'd used Gretchen as a model for Susan Heimrich's dog Colonel.

"I *thought* you must like dogs," Hildy said. "From Colonel."

Now that we had big dogs in common, she decided we ought to go walking. She went up to change and I heard her singing. I went to the telephone and began to make calls to real-estate agents, telling those who answered—I was too early for most of them—that I was taking the house off the market. One must sometimes make a large bet.

Hildy wore slacks and a sweater when she came down, and low-heeled walking shoes. She had come equipped, I thought. And she's one of the few women I've ever known who wear slacks well.

When we got outside, I was rather surprised to see Pammy loitering near the driveway in the bright sun. "Which cat is it?" Hildy asked. "I mean, who is she?"

I told her.

"Pammy, do you want to go walking with us?" Hildy called.

I thought to myself she still had a lot to learn about cats being different from dogs.

But Pammy, for some perverse reason, stuck close. That is, close for a cat outdoors—none of that *To heel* business. She danced around us, rollicking, wanting to be chased. She leaped up on a stone wall, and by graceful accident avoided the spot where poison ivy flourishes thickest. Cats don't get poison ivy; ladies do. I warned Hildy what to watch out for.

We walked along that stone wall first, the wall which parallels the driveway and has no real purpose now; which once fenced a farmer's field. Laurel planted along it was still brittle-brown. Beyond, the wall was a tangle of rambler roses—a dry and lifeless tangle. Ramblers are most tenacious plants; they can be pruned to the ground, to mere stubs of bushes, and come back again. But in early spring they never look as if they planned to. They surrender to winter, it has always seemed to me, more utterly than most green things. There was no sign of life in them that morning, under the slanting sunshine. I told Hildy what they were and that was probably needless. But I had met her in the city and still thought of her there, indigenous to the Village. There had always been flowers in her apartment, but that is a different thing.

"Those little red roses!" Hildy said.

I admitted, reluctantly, that the ramblers would be pink. I had been told, earlier, that pink was a color she loathed. I said that the ramblers had come with the land; the current owner was not to be held responsible.

Hildy said "Come off it. I never told you I loathed pink outdoors."

She had never seen hawthorn trees before and was enchanted with them, as I am, even bare and black: "Like Japanese prints."

But I still wanted to find something green for her: "Look, the daffodils are coming up."

They were coming up on the sunny side of the wall, in an area which had once been used as a cutting garden but which, as trees grew larger, had become too shady for flowers. The year before I had had it spaded and raked down and seeded to grass. That had not stopped the daffodils, which also are tenacious. Their shoots were coming up in clumps through the grass. Some of them looked as if they wished they had waited for warmer weather. Frost had nipped them. That didn't matter; they were still several weeks away from budding.

I told Hildy that in the meantime we would cut forsythia branches and take them inside to force. "So you'll have your yellow."

When we went across the terrace daffodils were

much taller in the narrow strip between flagstones and house where protection is greatest and sunlight strongest in the early spring, before the big ash tree shades it. A good many—too many—of the ash's smaller branches had broken off during the winter and littered the terrace and ground. I talk morosely about how long it had been dry in our part of the country. The autumn before—the fourth or fifth year of drought—the ash tree had yellowed early and shed its leaves in disconsolate fashion. The other ashes had too, but I told Hildy about this one because it was the most essential tree on the place, stretching up over the house, shading the terrace all summer.

"Can't we water it?" Hildy said.

I had been told the summer before, by the tree man, that it would be a fine idea to put the hose on that ash and let water run for twenty-four hours or so. I had asked what he thought that would do to a well —even a deep well with a good flow. "Wouldn't like to say," the tree man had told me. I told Hildy we'd see—that perhaps it would rain. I said, with no assurance, that it had to rain sometime.

Then suddenly I took in the way she had phrased her question. I quit worrying about the ash tree.

Pammy was still flickering in and out, around and around, as we walked back of the house, to a gap in another stone fence. It is a country of stone fences. We stood in the gap and looked at the field beyond.

Pammy rollicked ahead, glancing back at us with a "come on." Hildy waved to her absently. "What a lovely meadow."

I had never thought of it as a meadow, but only as a field. There are a good many blueberry bushes in the several acres of that field and they are spaced around—not in rows, but at pleasant intervals—as if some former owner had set them so. But they are wild blueberries, tart and flavorful as cultivated blueberries never are. The birds enjoy them very much.

I didn't want Hildy to go any farther right then. For reasons never clear to me, since the field is on a ridge, it is always mushy back there in the early spring. Standing in the gap we could see segments of another, distant, stone fence and I told her that beyond that wall there was a swampy area—a tangle of fallen trees and clutching bushes. And that there was supposed to be a brook.

Hildy said, "Supposed to be?"

I said it had probably dried up; that not for years had I fought my way to it.

"Take me down there some day. I'm crazy about brooks."

I felt like bashing through the underbrush and digging out the brook with my own bare hands. Fortunately, this feeling only lasted a moment. "Let's go back and find the clippers," I said. "We'll need them for the forsythia."

When we reached the house, Helen's car was parked beside the garage. And Pammy was sitting on the flagstones near the front door, waiting for us. She looked at us thoughtfully as we came around the house, along a strip in which tulips were tentatively beginning to poke up. I said, "Do you want to come in?" and rather hoped she'd say No. I hoped she would stay out the rest of the morning and exercise her claws on something more resistant than furniture.

Pammy had other ideas. She turned and faced the front door, waiting for it to be opened. I pushed it open and Pammy walked into the house in no special hurry. We followed her and Hildy stopped to take off a sweater. I hung it and my windbreak in the hall closet and turned back. Hildy was standing very still and very straight just where entrance hall changes to living room. Pammy, arched, was rubbing against Hildy's legs, stropping herself, as cats do. As cats do when they are confident.

Hildy stood very still, and for a moment I thought she was rigidly still. There are some people who do not like to have cats rub against their legs. It is one thing to look at a cat across a room and say, "How charming." Contact is quite another matter. There was nothing, that morning, to do but wait.

"Hello, Pammy," Hildy said, a little uncertainly.

Pammy lay down on her side by Hildy's feet and made a small, soft sound.

And Hildy crouched down beside her.

"Let her—" I began, and Hildy said, "I know. It's the same with dogs," and let Pammy smell her hand before she touched the cat. Pammy rolled over on her back and began to purr.

"She wants you to rub her belly," I said. "She's a great one to have her belly rubbed."

The lady sat down on the floor and gently stroked the expectant cat. Pam stretched long in delight, and purred more loudly.

"Pretty Pammy," Hildy said. "Pretty cat," and Pammy twisted a little to look up at her. "You have a darling face," Hildy told my cat. "You're a very pretty cat."

She spoke softly, tenderly, as one should to cats. One can say anything to cats, if the tone is right. The words one uses do not, for the most part, matter, although cats learn such words as are useful to them. "Pretty" is a good thing to call a cat, and Pammy, stretched to full length under a caressing hand, was very pretty that spring morning.

Hildy turned and looked up at me, but continued to stroke my cat.

I knew what she was wondering. I said, "I've never seen Pammy like this. She's always been friendly, but I never saw her surrender so utterly."

Nor had I, ever.

Hildy got up after a time, and Pammy, still

stretched out, watched her. Hildy began to walk
down the living room, her heels tapping on the tiles.
Pammy listened for a second or two. Then she was up
and trotting after the lady. When she got in front of
Hildy she lay down again, first on her side, as before.
Hildy stopped, since one does not step on a cat. Most
cats take rather undue advantage of this human hesi-
tancy. Hildy crouched again and stroked again.

Pammy rolled over on her back again. It was, I
realized, the sort of thing which might well go on
forever.

It did not, that morning, because Sherry appeared at the front door and mentioned that she was
there and Pammy coiled to her feet and trotted across
the room as if she intended to open the door for her
friend.

I went instead and pulled the door open. Sherry
started to come in and saw Hildy, who had got to her
feet when Pammy did and almost, it seemed to me, as
lithely.

Sherry turned and streaked away, heading, I assumed, around the house and toward the back door.
But it was never possible to be sure about Sherry.

"From now on, I'll have a way to tell them apart,"
Hildy said. "Sherry's the one that thinks I'm Lady
Dracula."

III

Worry

༜༜༜

I HADN'T MEANT to tell Hildy what I'd done about the house; not right then. On one thing—marriage—she was almost as skittish as Sherry. She was sitting on the sofa trying to brush pale cat hairs from her dark wool slacks, with no more success than one usually has. And she said, "Maybe I'll have to get some Siamese-colored clothes."

This sounded so promising I told her the house was no longer for sale. She took a gulping breath, as she does when she's startled, and said loving things. But she couldn't be rushed.

Helen came down from doing the bedrooms and sensed the emotional weather; she barely stopped to say good morning, before leaving us alone.

Pammy had no such scruples about interrupting an important moment. She leaped up and settled in, purring, on the lady. "It's a rather inadequate lap," Hildy said. "Like snuggling down on a wishbone."

I had already discovered she had some peculiar

notions of how she looked. For one thing, she thought she was bowlegged. She is not.

And Pammy made it clear she found nothing wrong with the lap. She wriggled in deeper, voluptuously.

"This is the first time I've ever been sat on by a cat," Hildy said. "It pulses."

I let that *it* pass. I heard Helen, at the back door, calling, "Sherry, here Sherry, come on now," in the soft coaxing tone that meant she had her in sight. So that was being taken care of; I could concentrate on the problem at hand—persuading a lady this was her home for keeps. Pammy, as silent partner, kept looking up adoringly. Hildy began asking questions: which cat was older; where had they come from. It was the first interest she had shown in the cats as individuals. Or maybe it was a female tactic to divert me from the subject we'd been on. If so, she chose a good way.

"Pammy was a present from a vet," I said. "Not Camuti. A vet near here. He knew we were looking for a cat after Martini died—this was about five years ago—and he phoned to say he had a fine Siamese. The owners were being transferred to South America and they wanted to be sure the cat would have a good home.

"I think they really had cared about Pammy. She had obviously been used to affection. And from the day we brought her here," I told Hildy, "she was so charmingly at home. She ate an enormous dinner; then I pointed and said, 'That's your toilet pan' and she nodded and went right over and used it. When she explored the house, she did it so gaily—she pranced and danced."

I thought she'd probably been brought up with children, because when friends brought children to the house she wasn't afraid of them, as most cats are. "Children puzzle and alarm cats who haven't known them early on," I said, wandering from the immediate subject as I commonly do when talking about cats. "At a guess, children seem to cats too large to be other cats or dogs, and too small to be humans.

"And maybe it was the children who let Pammy out when she was in heat, with inevitable results. During the first weeks we had her, we marveled over her appetite. Then I noticed she was filling out in a rather special way. I turned her over and her nipples were pink. So that was that. The vet was as surprised as we were. We took her back there to have her kittens, because we were going south for two months. But before we knew she was pregnant, we had picked out a six weeks' old kitten to be company for Pammy. We'd left her with the breeder and said we'd collect her when we came back from our holiday. She was too young to leave the mother cat anyway. But

if I'd known what was going to happen to her while
we were gone . . ."

Pammy turned her head and regarded me slit-
eyed, waiting for her name to be featured again.

So first I told what had happened to Pammy.
"The people who'd owned her assured the vet she had
had her shots. But she got enteritis, which used to be
fatal. And with Pammy it very nearly was. The vet
felt partly responsible, and he'd become so attached
to Pammy he was almost as upset as we were. He
wouldn't even charge us for her board, while she was
having oxygen and antibiotics. He wasn't too hopeful.
But one time he said, 'Pammy has a fighting heart.
She's trying so hard to live.' "

Hildy cupped Pammy's head in her hands.

"I felt so bitter, when we thought she was going
to die, that I wanted to write a letter to the local
paper, telling how a cat had been killed by carelessness. A beautiful dancing cat."

Pammy had pulled through. Without kittens.
"And when she came home and found Sherry here,
I've always thought that somehow she decided this
was her child. At first meeting they arched their
backs and bushed their tails and hissed. But within a
few hours they were close. And God knows Sherry
needed that. She was the most terrified cat I've ever
known, and still is."

When we'd picked Sherry out, I told Hildy, we'd

been rather surprised at the casual way the place was run: "The tom was a large, angry blue who lived in the basement of the house. And the two gentle seal-point queens were taken down to visit him whenever the need arose—theirs or the need for more salable kittens."

We had picked Sherry from a dozen charming Siamese kittens running uncertainly on a kitchen floor. "They were all so much alike even their mothers seemed to be confused. Either queen would gather to her any kitten within paw reach who needed food or chastisement." The woman who owned the place—I won't call it a cattery because it doesn't deserve the term—marked our kitten on the forehead with an indelible pencil, after we chose her from the litter. We had already named her Sherry. "Sherry Two, really," I told Hildy. "Sherry One and Gin were the daughters of Martini."

"Yes, I know," Hildy said impatiently. "I read Lockridge mysteries."

"And this is actually Pammy Two," I said. "Pammy One was ——"

"*Lockridge!*" she said. "Do you want me to tear out your hair?"

I pointed out nature had already taken care of that. Hildy said I had enough left to make a few good tufts. "This is the only Pammy I care about. Now go on."

I knew when not to argue. I told Hildy that when we went back to collect Sherry about six weeks later, the owner had brought out a cowering, terrified little thing that didn't even look like the lively kitten we'd chosen. But the indelible mark was there on her forehead, all right. "I shut her in a storeroom after you left," the woman said. "And kept her isolated the whole time so she wouldn't get attached to anybody else. I knew you wouldn't want that. Of course I put food in for her every day." Then she'd glanced at that poor, cowering kitten and said, "It may have made her a little shy."

"What a thing to do to her," Hildy said.

The result was the most desperately frightened cat I've ever been near. Or tried to get near. "When we brought Sherry here," I told Hildy, "she hid under a sofa and wouldn't come out for a week, while humans were around. When she finally came out, early one evening, it was only to race up the stairs and jump on that blanket chest outside your room. I think she thought it was a box she could hide in. When she discovered she couldn't get inside it, she cowered there and tried to bury herself in the wall."

Hildy was listening with gratifying intentness. "What did you do then?"

I had spent hours sitting beside the kitten, stroking her, talking to her. For a long time she shrank, terrified, from my touch. It was three or four hours before the little cat began to purr.

I remembered the moment of that first purring very well and as I told of it—of that strange small triumph—I suppose my voice changed. I am not sentimental about cats. A sentimentalist does not deserve a cat, or get along very well with one. But I suppose my voice did change. I said, "It was the deepest, most throbbing purr I'd ever heard."

Hildy had tears in her eyes. "You're the only man I've known who has the goodness, and tenderness, and patience . . ."

I was glad she hadn't known many cat owners. And even if I thought I didn't deserve a tenth of what she was saying, I wanted her to go on saying it. And thinking it. Because I knew that much more than a cat was involved.

Pammy knew it too; she went away in offended dignity, flouncing her tail.

The lady and I sat in a silence too sweet to break. But I was going to break it anyway, and press for a firm commitment. I began to think of the way I'd word the opening—something light but meaningful.

The silence was broken in a somewhat different fashion—by a pounding wham-bang. A sound so familiar to me I was surprised when Hildy jumped. "What is it—a tom-tom?"

It was Helen's own version of a tom-tom, beating a tin piepan with a large wooden mixing spoon to summon cats. Faraway cats. That meant Sherry hadn't accepted Helen's earlier invitation as I'd assumed.

"But it's such a pretty day," Hildy said, when I told her. "Why not let her stay out as long as she wants to?"

And I thought, Why not? But Pammy came in and swarmed over my feet, asking, in effect, What are you going to do about this? And Helen's tom-tom went on pounding, at intervals, for the next fifteen or twenty minutes. She was doing it much more for my sake than Sherry's. She knows the way I worry, often irrationally, when a cat doesn't come home. That's the main reason my cats get a third meal, although most people's cats are fed only twice a day, and many only once. Lunch is the incentive, the lure to inveigle them home. And then I try to see to it they don't get out again that day. Naturally cats do their wily best to circumvent this plan. Even two spayed females. But at least they do come home to lunch. And that way a lot of cat-calling is avoided. Particularly at night. Cat-calling and searching fifteen acres or so can be trying, to voice and flashlight batteries. I had had enough of that in the past. I wanted no more of it.

And my cats were used to the schedule. Sherry had been at the door, all ready to come in, until she saw Hildy. Even under the best conditions, Sherry was a strange, frightened cat. I began to worry; I have a natural talent for anticipating everyday disaster.

Pammy trotted from front door to terrace door, then back again to the front, peering out, doing her routine of, Where is my wandering child? Now she came and clawed my pants leg. I said ouch; so did my conscience.

I got up reluctantly and said I'd go out and give Sherry a call.

Hildy said in a rather muted voice, "You think it would be better if I didn't come along?" She was looking out the window.

It was, most certainly, better for my purpose if she did not come along. I said, "Get your coat."

We walked first toward the back field—meadow —because it was a favorite hunting ground of Pammy's and Sherry's. Cats are supposed to be creatures of habit, but they change their habits without warning humans. And since Sherry, of all the cats I've ever had, was the most wildly unpredictable, I could never even guess what she'd do. All I could do was start somewhere and hope my voice would carry. "Sher-ry —here, Sher-ry."

My vocal chords had been toughened by years of cat-calling; also by projecting my voice to women's clubs, in the days before microphone resonance. "Sherry—here, Sher-ry."

The sun had gone under, suddenly. It was much

colder and the ground felt dank underfoot. With part of my mind I noticed the top of the willow was sickly yellow—probably dying of thirst. Hildy kept roaming off to examine trees and bushes close to, touching and sniffing rather like a child or a puppy. She had pretty much forgotten why we'd come out; I hadn't. It wasn't like Sherry to stay out when the day turned raw; she was almost as much a fair-weather cat as Martini had been. Not quite, though. Martini would take a look outside after breakfast and if it was raining she'd retire for the day. It might quit raining and clear up in an hour, but Martini always gave the whole day up if the start looked bad.

"Gin was the only cat that loved walking in the rain," I said. Thinking about Ginny made me worry more lucidly, and shout even louder. "Here Sher-ry—Sher-ry."

Hildy said she'd never heard of cats being expected home for lunch. "You fuss too much." And she teased me about the way I can worry over nothing.

I agreed that I was a champion worrier. But this time I had some reason. I said country cats ran all sorts of risks. "Ginny fell into an abandoned well somebody hadn't got around to covering. She drowned. We went around searching for weeks."

Hildy said, "Oh, I'm so sorry." With real sorrow.

It had happened in broad daylight. "We had people for lunch on the terrace—too many people for

Gin and Martini. They went roving across the road. Martini came back soaking wet and licked herself dry. But Ginny never came back. A boy found her body eventually. I always supposed they both fell into the well, probably when they were chasing each other. And Martini must have stood on Ginny's shoulders and jumped out."

"You mean really?" Hildy said in a shocked voice. "She stood on her daughter's shoulders and let her daughter drown? No dog would do that."

I said hastily that I had no way of knowing. Probably not really. It would have been very like Martini, who was self-centered even for a cat. But I regretted having said it. In some odd way Hildy's acceptance of cats was coming to be involved with an acceptance much more vital.

When we circled around to the right of the house, I realized the wind had shifted to the northeast. We might be in for some rough weather. "Here Sher-ry— Sher-ry." I was getting hoarse. Hildy began calling too. Her voice is light; I didn't think it likely to carry to distant feline ears, and, on the whole, I hoped it wouldn't.

"Sher-ry," she called, high and sweet. "Sher-ry, where are you?"

And Sherry, from a distance, answered. She answered in the voice of a cat who is up a tree and doesn't like any part of it.

Hildy said, "Over there, I think," and started off. She has an almost infallible instinct for turning in the wrong direction. This was the first demonstration rurally. I hauled her back and followed my ears, calling as we went. Now Sherry always answered. "Yow-*ow*, yow-*ow*." The closer we got, the more she screamed. "Ow-ow-*ow*—yahaow." She was really making a pitch about it.

We followed the sound to a big maple tree near the wall which divides my acres from a neighbor's. Then we tilted our heads back and followed the sound up a tree to a cat staring down at us. She was a good way up, entirely secure on a thick branch. And screeching like a banshee. Or a Siamese cat.

"Can't she get down?" Hildy asked me. "Do we call the fire department or something?"

I said we'd do no such thing. Having worried myself to a frenzy, I felt like a parent who's relieved enough to be sore. "She's quite capable of coming down if she wants to."

This wasn't entirely fair. A cat's claws are perfectly curved for climbing up. But they are no good for coming down. A cat has to back down out of a tree and there is a trick turn at the start of a backdown. A cat starts headfirst, to see where he is going, which is entirely reasonable. He jumps to lower branches. But when he runs out of lower branches and comes to trunk he has, with momentarily no firm hold, to twist around. No cat likes this much. Mother cats have to do a lot of wheedling to kittens, explaining the trick. Sometimes they have to climb up and demonstrate. Some cats are better at it than others; Sherry had never been as expert as Pammy. There is nothing a human can do to help, short of a ladder. I didn't have a tall ladder.

Even if I'd had one, I would have hesitated to use it. Years before, at Lost Lake, I'd rescued one young cat from a tree, climbing a ladder in the best tradition of S.P.C.A. Before I could quite get my hands on the cat, she had leaped onto my shoulder, clinging, clawing in desperation. I was wearing a thin tennis shirt at the time.

Now I was twenty years older and wiser, wearing a well-padded windbreak as I exhorted Sherry to be a brave, resourceful cat. "All you have to do is start. Come on, Sherry. Come on down and get your lunch." I kept on with this pep talk till I noticed that Hildy was hunching inconspicuously into her lightweight coat, shivering. And I remembered how sick she had been with the sinus infection. I insisted we go indoors. "As soon as Sherry finds she's not the center of attention, she'll come down." I didn't altogether believe this myself. I was counting more on the fact that cats dislike wind. A dislike I share. And this wind was almost strong enough to blow away a small-boned lady.

I built a fire for us, although it wasn't really necessary at noon. We were basking there, with our drinks, when Hildy said, "I'm glad you aren't the kind who cares more about cats than people." She said it thoughtfully; I had a gratified feeling I'd passed some kind of test, like killing a dragon. After that I was careful not to go to the door too often.

But I didn't relax, really, till I heard Helen open the back door and say, "All right, Sherry. . . . Yes, I know it's a cruel world, but you don't have to take it that hard. Eat your lunch."

We ate ours later, peacefully. Pammy had considerately gone upstairs with Sherry, to let her sleep it off. Helen, even more considerately, didn't come in to collect our coffee cups. I finally took them out to the kitchen when I saw, with astonishment, that my watch had rushed to almost four o'clock. Helen leaves around midafternoon, unless there are guests for dinner. And I wanted this guest all to myself, for reasons that were clear to everybody except cats.

Helen had her bird book spread open on the drainboard, and she was looking out the window over the sink. She had lived in the house, with the cats, while I was gone, and had put up two feeders strung on wires between trees. I had discovered she'd paid for the big bag of wild-bird seed herself. She had refused to let me reimburse her: "It's my hobby—not yours." But I had told her that from now on the birds would eat on me.

"Nothing much but starlings today," she said.

"And I just heard a rain crow. What's the weather going to do tonight?"

I told her what I thought; I may not know much about feathered objects, but I do know something about wind shifts.

Helen listened carefully. But she waved aside my apology for holding her up so late. She said, "We won't worry about schedules right now. This is a special time." She was smiling; and I liked the way she said "special."

"I didn't have much to do last week," she said. (She had merely washed every window in the house, waxed every floor, and held off real-estate agents.) "So I cooked up some extra things ahead and put them in the freezer. Veal birds and spaghetti and lamb curry. In case you don't want to eat out every night while Miss Dolson is here."

I had taken Hildy, the first evening, to an inn I like; to which, during empty years, I had gone almost nightly. And I'd introduced her to the owner, who, when one's luck is in, is also the chef. Hildy told him she'd heard what a superb cook he was, and our luck ran high—a beef bourguinionne with the master's touch. Also a fine hollandaise for the fresh asparagus. After we'd finished dinner, the owner had bought us a drink and sat with us, and said I was looking much better than I had for a long time. He said it was evident that Key West had agreed with me. He is a perceptive man. "Or something has," Walter Tode added.

There was another inn I wanted to take Hildy to —Fox Hill on the far side of Ridgefield—where a pianist played the kind of songs we like best—Gershwin and Rodgers and Kern—played them as they ought to be played, without the trills that bury a good tune in ruffles.

But on a raw night like this one shaping up—I watched Helen put new candles in the silver candlesticks. And I thought about her veal birds and spaghetti and lamb curry. And I thought about Hildy saying, "But I'm not domestic. I can't even cook a real meal." It was one of her why-I'd-make-an-awful-wife tenets.

"I like her," Helen said. "She's right for you." She was giving me her blessing. And she is one of the friends whose opinion I value and trust. Not that anybody's opinion of Hildy—good or bad—could have changed my own. But I was pleased.

So was Hildy, when I reported. "Before we came up here, I pictured your housekeeper as somebody like Mrs. Danvers in *Rebecca*—alpaca apron, dangling keys, and implacable. Boy, was I relieved to see Helen."

I remembered *Rebecca* very clearly. I remembered, especially, that it was the new wife who had been terrified of Mrs. Danvers. The signs and portents seemed bright.

As Helen drove off, we started out to cut forsythia; I sent Hildy back to add another layer, a sweater, under her coat. And I stood outside waiting, examining the hemlock to see if red spider had done much damage. Suddenly an apparition streaked past me—a long, lean Siamese cat. Except that it was no apparition—it was Sherry. "Damn it to hell," I yelled.

Hildy heard me. She was standing in the doorway looking bewildered. "I'm so sorry. I just turned back to get my gloves, after I'd opened the door. The cat was clear up on the landing. She didn't seem at all interested in getting out. She was *yawning*."

Hildy had been conned—by a cat. I assured her that it wasn't her fault, that experienced cat owners have been conned, often. Including me.

Sherry had disappeared instantly. And I knew better than to chase her. You can tell by the way a cat runs whether she wants to be chased and caught. Sherry may have wanted to be chased, but she hadn't the smallest intention of being caught.

I clipped forsythia and shouted at intervals, and Hildy kept saying how sorry she was. "I didn't know which cat it was or I might have been more careful. Now you'll really worry in earnest. I hate to have you worried."

I told her gallantly that I wasn't at all worried. I said the surest way to get Sherry home was for us to go up and take naps. "Then she'll climb up the pear tree and onto the roof of the garage and on over so she can yell at my window."

When Hildy and I discovered, soon after we met, that we are both late-afternoon nappers, it had seemed like a fascinating coincidence, as fascinating as discovering we both loathed cucumbers. Every time we'd met since, we had tended to stay up later and later. So I can honestly say that our taking naps had turned out to be more important than our not taking cucumbers.

Hildy said, "Will you really go up and sleep?"

I promised to try. And I tried. I shut Pammy out of the big bedroom, where she'd been having her afternoon nap, and I lay down and shut my eyes. And worried. Partly about two-legged matters. And about poison garden pellets which some fool newcomer to the area might have strewn around to kill marauding raccoons, rabbits, or woodchucks. My long-time neighbors along this road all keep pets, and wouldn't take a chance on any dog or cat getting poisoned. But city people who garden in a weekend way are inclined to believe they can cure nature's ills instantly, drastically, "to gain prompt relief." There were two new houses within a mile; Sherry might be the poison victim of either. But to get that far, she might have first gone down to the main road beyond our driveway, Route 123; I had seen too many smashed bodies of animals strewn along it. Cats are so fast they know they can get away from any moving object like a man or a horse. But even bright cats often find it hard to believe a car can go so much faster. And they'll run across a highway with what seems like a safe margin —and die.

I have considerable experience in thinking up ways for people to be killed, and relatively few ways for cats. But if I can't think up some new kind of doom for a missing cat, I can always use the old worries over and over, with imaginative twists.

The past two lonely years had sharpened my sense of anxiety—about cats, catching trains, and, most of all, about my own future. I couldn't quite believe that my luck had come back; that Hildy meant the loving things she said. And why should she marry me, anyway? She must have known dozens of men— if they hadn't changed her mind on marriage, how could I, over sixty, with not all my hair and teeth?

I can't remember precisely which worry I was on when heels tapped in that quick, almost running way. Hildy was awake. And singing. Not in words, and not exactly humming either. All I could catch was what sounded like "Da ooma guppa ooma da." But I recognized the tune—"I've Got My Love to Keep Me Warm."

I leaped off the bed refueled with positive energy. I wanted to lay the fire and get out ice and make sure the veal birds were thawing fast enough.

And see what Helen had done about a vegetable. And feed Pammy. And take another look around for Sherry before Hildy came down.

I was a dynamo of hope.

But by eight o'clock it was raining hard. And still no sign of Sherry. For a while I put up quite a good front. I remembered to find a bottle of wine; it was the only one in the house, and a split at that. Red, so there was none of that nonsense about whether a red or a white was proper. I simmered the veal birds in cream. And I lit the candles. Rain whipped against the wide windows in the dining room, and cold seeped in through the glass till I pulled the curtains to shut out the night.

It's a tribute to Helen's cooking that we both ate two helpings. The atmosphere was not exactly conducive to gracious dining. The way I half listened to the lady and half listened for a cat may have contributed to the strain. And my running to the door every five or ten minutes to call, "Sher-ry." Each time I shouted for Sherry, Pammy would answer. From upstairs, or the kitchen. This added to the air of confusion.

I tried to read some poetry to Hildy: the lovely " 'It's morning,' Senlin says" sequence of Conrad Aiken's—but Pammy fixed that, too. She kept bouncing like a ping-pong ball from one lap to another. When she was told to go away, she went as far as the nearest chair and sharpened her claws. Then she worked off her resentment—k-k-kr-r-r-r-r-r-rip . . . k-k-k-k-kr-r-r-r-rip. The sound of a cat clawing upholstery is not the ideal accompaniment for a lyric rendering of poetry.

When Hildy thought I wasn't looking, she put her hand to her forehead in a press-the-pain-away gesture. She said it was just a bit of sinus, and I preferred to think that poetry and caterwauling had nothing to do with it. I said again that I wanted to take her away to a decent climate, the next winter. "If we can swing it."

Somehow we got into a ridiculous argument about whether it would be good to have a million dollars. I said I'd be delighted if somebody gave me a million (which was the only way I'd get it). Hildy said it would be "simply horrible"; a million dollars would entail all kinds of new demands on one's time. "And the rich people I've met never seemed happy." I said I would be happy. We argued until Hildy became so worked up she said she didn't even want me to *want* a million dollars. I said, Well, I did; I refused to retract. Hildy took this crass attitude very hard. She looked so flushed I put my hand on her forehead: heated. I gave her two aspirin. She was still so cross at me for accepting a mythical million dollars that she said she only wanted a smidgin of brandy. Her word —*smidgin*. I do not think it is suitable for brandy.

7 *1*

She had long since stopped apologizing for letting Sherry out. She has a short attention span for apologizing. So do I.

Around midnight, she said she was going to bed. "If I'm getting a cold or something, I don't want to give it to you."

I said I never got colds.

She said I sounded revoltingly smug.

I said, Well, I got indigestion. "I've got it right this minute, if you want to know. I'm not supposed to eat uncooked greens."

This wasn't the most fortunate thing to say, because Hildy had made the salad. Or at least she'd tossed it, very prettily, with Helen's oil and vinegar dressing.

She was decently sympathetic. But she said, "If you could only stop worrying about Sherry, your stomach would feel better." Which was probably true. "I'm sure he'll come home safe."

I pointed out, rather sharply, that Sherry was a she.

Hildy said, "But she acts more like a man."

I said, "You're not making sense."

Hildy said, "No, I'm not. I wonder why I said that." She's inclined to be honest—sometimes disarmingly so.

When we said goodnight, she forgave me for never catching cold.

I said I'd fold up as soon as I'd banked the fire. I had kept it roaring all evening, to the point that I'd used up every log in the wood closet under the stairs. I'd wanted to be sure Hildy was warm enough; the fact that she loved the fireplace—and fires—may have increased my zeal.

I kicked the burning logs apart, to calm them down, and closed the mesh screen. And sat down again, alone, to worry. Pammy came down and sat beside me. She wasn't fussing at me any longer about Sherry's absence. Being a realistic cat, she must have understood there was nothing more I could do right then. I didn't want to go out into the cold rainy night any more than she did.

And I wouldn't have left Hildy alone in the house. There had been a series of burglaries in our area. Owners of houses always left their lights on when they went away, to show they were home. I didn't think this fooled burglars much. And if Hildy heard a crash and got up to find out why I'd fallen over a chair—this was a new enough worry to distract me, temporarily, from worrying about Sherry. I went around checking all the doors, to be sure they were locked. It seemed to me no burglar would come out in that rain.

And no cat would stay out in it, when she had a home to come to. Sherry must have been hurt. Or she had gone deep into the swampy stretches and been bogged in treacherous mud.

Around one o'clock I went to bed. And slept in a nagging, surface way. Once I came awake to an owl's hoot. *Owls they whinny down the night.* A hoot owl had swooped down on Sherry and carried her off. I dozed again and dreamed I was on the edge of a cliff, flapping my arms at a hoot owl. I fell. Either that or the owl pushed me. I woke in a cold sweat.

Then I heard Pammy talking. I knew that tone. I ran downstairs and found Pammy at the front door, as I'd supposed she would be. Sherry was outside it, a pale blur pressed against the glass panel of the door. Both of them were talking loudly about what terrible things people do to cats.

Sherry came in; she was entirely dry.

IV

Hunting

"I took a whole sleeping pill," Hildy said. She was looking very fresh and rested. The sun had come out earlier, but the lady hadn't emerged till around ten, when my fog lifted officially.

I told her about Sherry. She seemed pleased but not inordinately. She said I worried too much, and was I through with the front section of the *Times*?

But she insisted on doing the breakfast dishes instead of leaving them for Helen. "I rather like this dishwasher—I feel more at home with it. Whenever I go near one in friends' houses, the machine acts as if it would throw the dishes right back at me. This one seems yielding."

It was over fifteen years old, almost as old as the house, and it leaked. I watched a yellow robe drift past the rotted linoleum at the right-hand side of the dishwasher where the leak was worst. And I willed the machine, silently, to hang on for another few months, till I could get other things to mesh. It gnashed its gears and groaned and thrashed; but it didn't spit.

We stood at the kitchen window and looked at the birds around the feeders. Helen's bird book was still on the sill. "Bird books have never done me much good," I said. "By the time I find a suitable picture the bird I'm trying to identify has always flown away. And I can't remember what it looked like."

Hildy said she was baffled by people who leaped up at dawn and crouched under bushes with binoculars. "I'll never be a bird watcher. I'm a bird glancer." I was glad to find she knew even less than I did.

The sun had brought out a much better variety than the day before; even I recognized cardinals. But that morning I saw something I had never seen before: the male cardinal would pick up a seed, run over to the female, and feed it to her, beak to beak, nuzzling.

Hildy was charmed. For one wild moment I wondered if Helen had coached the birds to stage the scene for the lady.

Hildy said she'd never seen one so brilliantly red. "He blazes."

"He's always more brilliant in the spring—it's mating season." This was one of the few pieces of birdlore I knew.

"You mean they only have one mating season a *year?*" Hildy said. "Poor devils."

Two blue jays were poised on each end of a branch like porcelain mantelpiece ornaments. I rather like blue jays, although I know this view is not widely popular, especially with other birds. When one swooped over to the feeder, all the little birds fled to the shelter of a bare forsythia bush. The jay began furiously to bill the seeds, knocking off the ones he thought unworthy, keeping the sunflower seeds to crack on a nearby branch.

"Robins aren't nearly as handsome," Hildy said. "But they've built up such an image—the spring on the wing, harbinger thing."

The only robin in sight was looking for worms and not finding them. I would have thought it was too early in the year for worms, and I was not entirely convinced that robins know best. Robins are not especially bright, even as birds go. I told Hildy that, years before, a robin of my acquaintance had dueled violently with his reflection in the shining hubcap of a car; had banged into it and knocked himself out; had staggered to wing and again assailed with fury this trespasser on his staked preserves. I had finally had to move the car.

"Maybe somebody watching a robin invented *birdbrain*," Hildy said.

A large squirrel whizzed up a tree, followed by its tail; I've always thought squirrels come in sections. Then Pammy came across the winter-gray, winter-brown grass toward the house, and birds scattered. Pammy didn't pay any attention to them, which was fine. I had been a bit uneasy, seeing her come home so early.

As soon as I let her in, she trotted right over and rolled at Hildy's feet in adoration. She had come home to see the lady. And she took over the lady, following the clicking heels wherever they went, then rolling over again to be stroked. I began to feel rather left out. I told Hildy, "You needn't pay all that much attention to her."

And I urged Pammy to go out again and play in the nice fresh air. But she wouldn't leave until Hildy went up to the guest room to work and shut the door firmly.

I was all for Hildy's working in my house, because I wanted every part of her life to be transplanted here. And work was a very important part. Hildy had told me she'd once been involved with a man who sounded to me like a blowhard out of Ibsen: "He kept trying to cut me down, and belittle anything I did," Hildy said. "He kept trying to knock me off-balance so I couldn't work at all. I stopped seeing him." She had told me several times, "You're so different. You only want to build me up."

But, that morning, my feelings on this were rather a mixed bag. Hildy was working on notes for talks she was to give in several colleges the next week.

And then spend a week at the college she herself had gone to, Allegheny, in western Pennsylvania, to take part in seminars on writing. I had been dismayed: "Cancel it all," I'd said. "I just got home. You can't go away now."

She said she had made the commitments before she even met me. "I told you in a letter that I was going. I said I could only visit you a few days. And I'll only be away two weeks. You were away thirty-nine days and nights. You're a fine one to talk."

At times I think there is something to be said for the double standard. But I am not the man to say it.

I went up to my office and lay on the couch and scratched through my mind to see if there was a plot gimmick hidden under anything. That, at any rate, was what I told myself I was doing. My mind wandered even more than it usually does in a plotting session. I got up and looked out the side window, toward the field with the old asparagus bed. Hildy liked asparagus; I must get the bed worked right away. I phoned Mr. Salvestrini who does plowing and such. He was out but his wife said she would have him call.

I phoned the Weather Bureau and heard what I already guessed—wind shift to the north, a chance of light snow. I always like to know that the Weather Bureau and I see eye to eye, even when we see something lousy. Snow was the last thing I wanted. And what if a frost knocked off the daffodils I'd promised

Hildy? I went into the big bedroom and looked out the windows facing east, to see how the branches were blowing. Sherry and Pammy were sitting side by side on the stone wall that separates my land from the Di Montes'. In that motionless pose, they looked nobly beautiful. I happened to know that what they were doing was making faces at the Di Monte dog, securely chained outside the garage. He was howling with rage and frustration. Mike Di Monte had told me, "Your cats always make sure he's chained and then they sit there and leer till they nearly drive him wild."

I had thought vaguely that Sherry might have picked the wrong time to leer, the day before, and that the Di Monte dog had got even, at last, and chased her up the tree. But he hadn't hung around to bark. And Sherry hadn't acted like a cat who's mad at a dog; she had acted like a cat who is mad at humans.

One cat left the wall as I watched. Sometimes it's hard to tell one seal-point Siamese from another, but even at that distance I knew it was Sherry from the long, lean way she stalked, and the way she slanted a little downhill because her hind legs are longer. Pammy waited a few seconds, probably for one last leer, then ran in her buoyant high-tailed way, down to the back field-meadow.

When I thought of the affinity between Pammy

and the lady, I felt quite cheered. And the plot I cooked up had nothing to do with mysteries. I most decidedly didn't want any mystery about it—I wanted everything clear with Hildy before she went off. She had said she wanted us to have dinner at home again, "Because tonight we could really settle down and appreciate it. And maybe both cats would sit with us and watch the fire."

I knew what would be missing from that picture —Sherry. But I intended to see to it she wasn't missing beyond the first floor. Our fire would blaze late—and bright. I must bring in a new load of wood from the half cord stacked behind the garage. I hurried downstairs, and was just going out when I heard Hildy moving around. Not heels tapping; only her mules and dress-up shoes had that clicketing sound. But even in flat heels she moved like nobody else. The wood could wait. I got out ice, filled the thermos bucket, and had everything ready on top of the chest that serves as a bar in the living room. I just had time to fill Helen in on Sherry's night out when I heard Hildy come out of her room, hurry along the balcony corridor to the landing, and start down. The front door is at the foot of the stairs, and, as I waited for Hildy, Pammy appeared on the other side of the door with something in her mouth—something still wriggling. She wanted to bring it in and show off her catch and be praised for it. She mentioned this in the

muffled tones of a cat who has a mouth full of chipmunk.

Chipmunks have always seemed to me quite
charming, spunky little things. And I doubted that it
would make Hildy view the killing more calmly if I
told her this catch was quite a trick to come by.

I had bent down fast as I opened the door, one
hand spread against my cat. Pammy, knowing what I
was up to, tried to dodge in. She intended to take the
chipmunk to her new lady, her adored. And I intended she shouldn't. I managed to stop her—the
margin narrow. Once outside, I had to wrestle with
her and the by then quite dead chipmunk. I won out,
finally, as I would not have done with many cats. I
had never been able to take anything away from
Sherry, partly because when she had prey it was even
more impossible to catch her. Unlike most cats, she
did not bring game home. She did not trust humans
enough to share any such triumph with them.

I put Pammy's booty in a refuse can in the garage, and clanged the top back on. Pammy was furious. She had gone to a lot of trouble, I knew, to bring
us a chipmunk. She went off at a slow, sullen walk,
her tail swishing.

Hildy had come outside. "What was that she had
in her mouth?"

I thought of saying, "Just a muddy piece of
wood." But I swallowed and said, "A chipmunk."

"Good for Pammy," the lady said. "I don't like chipmunks. They scuttle like rats. And a tame one bit my Grandmother Brown when she was a little girl. On the finger, right to the bone. She always warned us never to trust a chipmunk."

I recovered my powers of speech; I called Pammy back and told her what a clever cat, what a great hunter she was. This didn't altogether make up for my earlier boorishness. But when Hildy knelt down and stroked her under the chin, Pammy melted. When we went back indoors, she took only one last, wistful look at the garbage can before following. The lady was more enticing than any chipmunk. And easier to corner. Easier for a cat, that is.

While we had a drink, I told Hildy about the time I had seen three of my cats form a semicircle around a chipmunk which danced in rage, reared high, and chattered in fury. It was one of the few times I had ever seen cats hunt together. "Mostly they're loners too," I said. I had assumed, watching this concentration of cats, that the spunky, tiny creature had had it.

But the cats seemed baffled by so much animosity in so small a body. They crouched and swished their tails. Perhaps each waited for another to move in; they may have been confused by their own ganging up. It is possible, also, that each cat thought one of the others had staked out the chipmunk. A cat's prey is that cat's prey; other cats may watch but not intervene.

"What happened to the chipmunk?"

"Got away. Made a run for it and went into a dry stone wall. There are almost always cracks in them big enough to hide a chipmunk."

The cats had moved when there was no longer any point to it. They had—oh, not quite had—bumped their heads against the wall. They separated then, and searched for chipmunk. So far as I know, they never found that one.

Hildy said, well, rats were spunky too, and that didn't mean she had to admire rats. "Once I thought of getting a house in the country—but that's the one place I wouldn't want to live alone, because of mice and rats. I don't think I'm a timid kind of woman, but when it comes to mice and rats, I'm a squealing idiot."

This was splendid news for me and my cats. "Pammy and Sherry wouldn't even let a field mouse come near here," I said.

Pammy's ears twitched in agreement. I described how they patrolled the garage every morning. "Together or in shifts. Sometimes I think they've worked out a sentry schedule." The garbage truck came only once a week. "If it weren't for my cats, we'd be overrun with rats. And we don't have a one."

Both Pammy and I lapped up the lady's approval. Having stumbled on this bonanza—like falling down a hole into an unworked gold mine—I made the most of it. I talked about the historic association between cats and people that, so far as we know, began in Egypt, the country of granaries, where cats were hired to catch rodents. "Cats became gods there."

That may have been incidental to their eating mice in granaries, but I am not above slanting a story. I went on about these godlike creatures, the true friends of mankind.

The phone rang. I dislike answering phones, and whenever possible I get somebody else to do it. Helen took the call on the phone in my office. She came downstairs to deliver the message.

"That was Mr. Salvestrini, about cleaning up the asparagus bed. He said to tell you he had his arm clawed by a neighbor's cat and it's all swollen and infected. He just came from the doctor's and he won't be able to work for a while. It's his right arm. The cat clawed it clear up to the elbow."

"Oh," I said. "Thank you, Helen."

"You're welcome," Helen said. As an exit line.

Hildy said one of their Airedales—Trouble the Second—had bitten a postman. "A motorcycle cop almost ran him down one time, so he wanted to bite anything in uniform to get even. We had to give him away to a farmer."

I accepted this balm gratefully. I said I would

try to find somebody else to clean the asparagus bed. "So we'll have fresh asparaus by May."

Later I took Hildy out to the back porch to point out the location of the bed. "It starts on a line with this gap and runs about fifteen feet. I'll show you to-morrow."

Hildy started to say something.

"Get back!" I shouted. "Here comes Sherry. Get out of sight—don't let her see you or she'll never come in."

Hildy disappeared—fast. Sherry, after a cautious look around, came into the kitchen. I praised her. And fed her. And went to find Hildy.

"I thought maybe you'd like me to have lunch in my room," she said. "So Sherry won't be upset again. Tell her that Lady Dracula is leaving tomorrow."

I became rather emotional.

Hildy relented and said her leaving had nothing to do with Sherry. "I wasn't going to tell you till after lunch—but I discovered this morning I'd left half my notes in town." She said she couldn't write the talks without them. And she had to do some shopping be-fore she left New York.

I knew she had four more days and I was deter-mined she'd stay till zero hour in the country. I pleaded; I lost my temper; I sounded like a character out of Ibsen. No, more out of Chekhov. I got nowhere. Then I said if she absolutely must go into town tomorrow, I would drive her in and stay at the hotel till she took off. Hildy said that would be fine. And she said she'd really much rather have stayed.

My plans for that evening seemed even more vital. I made a mental check list. Hildy had voted for spaghetti because she's fond of Italian food, and maybe, too, because I had told her Helen's spaghetti was one of the few dishes that had tempted me to eat during a period when there seemed no point in eating. We would need some other things; I consulted Helen who said, "You might buy a whole roast chicken for the cats and shut them up with it in the downstairs guest room." She was joking—some. She said, "Miss Dolson is happy here. You can tell. And everything seems so cheerful when she's around." She wasn't joking then.

I wanted Hildy to see the village, so that afternoon we went in on our errands and walked up and down Main Street. Ridgefield, Connecticut, is a charming small town. Main Street is also a numbered highway. But a good many of the big white houses of an older time still line the road and some of them were there when British redcoats and Americans in homespun fought with muskets up and down a muddy turnpike. Fought, I think, inconclusively; none of the several battles of Ridgefield seems to have had special bearing on the outcome of the Revolutionary War. Some friends of mine, I told Hildy as we walked around, had an old house there. Not on Main Street. Sometime we would go to see them, I told her. One of the chimneys of their old house had a black stripe painted around it. It had been so when my friends bought the house, and when they repainted they kept the stripe around the white chimney. They lived in the house for some years before they discovered that the black stripe once had meant that the people who owned the house were loyal to the crown and the house was not for burning.

We went into Gristede's and bought an alligator pear to go with the spaghetti, and French bread. They knew me in Gristede's, of course. We went into the liquor store a few doors away, to get wine. They knew me, conceivably too well, in the liquor store. They looked at the lady with interest, as people had in Gristede's. We went to the Ridgefield Hardware Store on Helen's instruction: "We need a new lamp for the guest room," Helen had told me. "Get Miss Dolson to help you pick out one she likes." I had been rather reluctant to carry out this errand because I am anti-shopper by nature. But Hildy took to it with a housewifely gleam that surprised me. She even asked prices, something I am very poor at. She told the owner, Ed Rabin, that he had a really wonderful lot of shades. By the time we settled on one the place seemed quite full of people who greeted me. It seemed to me on that afternoon we ran into rather more people who knew me, by sight at least, than was usually true. They looked with interest at the lady—the small, quick lady—beside me. When one lives for fifteen years or so in the vicinity of a village one comes to be recognized. And, of course, a little wondered about. A good many people knew what had happened to me more than two years before. They had seen me walking around alone.

The wind shifted back to the northeast as we walked Ridgefield together, and freshened a little and the sun began to dim behind thickening clouds. The temperature started down. The Weather Bureau and I had been right; there was a high chance of snow. The first flakes came down as we walked back to the car. This made me think boldly of still another purchase. There is a place in one of the shopping centers that sells ski clothes and tweed things. I asked Hildy if she wouldn't like to go in with me and pick out a coat: "A country-warm."

Hildy said, We-e-el-l-l-l-l-l, no, she wasn't sure she'd use a country coat enough to justify buying one. I said I wanted to charge it. Hildy said, almost fiercely, "I have my own money." That ended that. She said she would be warm enough in the car.

It wasn't warm in the car, which was ten years old and had developed senility of the heater. But it was warm in the house. Pammy was at the door; she rubbed against Hildy's ankles and rolled over in a near-swoon of ecstasy. Hildy sat on the floor with her. The heat in the downstairs of the house comes from hot water in pipes in a concrete slab under the tile, and it had begun to warm up, on orders from the thermostat. Hildy noticed the floor was warm and I explained to her how it worked; how, in hot summer weather, the cold water standing in the pipes cooled the floor as now the hot water was beginning to heat it. It made a good floor for cats, as well as for people, I told her. The cats always liked to stretch out on the cool floor as soon as they came in on a hot day. And now Pammy was warming herself, although it looked to me as if she were drawing more warmth from lady than floor.

I had seen Sherry lying on the stair landing as we came in. That spot was directly above the furnace and warm as a heating pad. She had bolted the minute she saw the lady. I thought she was still upstairs, but I was hyper-careful about closing the front door behind me when I went out for wood. Hildy offered to help me; I told her I didn't want her to get cold. It was snowing enough to show on the ground. "You keep Pammy happy till I come back. This is man's work."

I went to the woodpile behind the garage and brushed snow off the top logs. I piled logs on the wheelbarrow, then more logs—and more. What my grandmother used to call "A lazy man's load."

The wheelbarrow, when I picked it up, seemed even more rickety than I remembered it. Being out another winter hadn't done it any good. It wobbled as I wheeled it between Helen's car and the pear-tree island at the corner of the garage; it twisted in my hands as if it wanted to rid itself of its burden.

I wheeled it in front of the house and thought that if I merely let go the handles and let the barrow drop it probably would fall apart. So I let it down slowly, gently.

And sharp, excruciatingly sharp, pain lashed through my back. I swore explosively and got into the house.

Hildy was standing up by the time I had falteringly walked the length of the living room. She looked at me anxiously.

"Sprained my back," I told her. She said, "Oh, no!" And led me tenderly to a sofa.

I told her I had done it before and that it was nothing serious, and that at the moment it hurt like hell.

Then I sat, very carefully, and watched as Hildy and Helen brought logs in from the barrow to the wood closet, one log at a time.

V

Setback

⚜⚜⚜

I HAD TO BE helped up and down like a tottery old man. Hildy was so concerned she wanted to call a doctor.

I said a doctor would only prescribe heat, and I'd never found that heat helped with a sprain. All I had to do was sit still for a few days. The idea of being immobilized on Hildy's last evening—not even able to take her into New York the next day—made me frantic. I was anxious to make her understand it wasn't the heavy load that had done me in—or age and decrepitude; it was simply my own carelessness. I told her that years before I had sprained my back lifting the lightest of little tables. Sprained it because I should have used my legs, not my back. What it came to, a doctor friend of mine had once told me, was that one "lifted his own weight." I had never entirely understood this explanation, but it had always fascinated me.

"Like a body displacing its own weight in water?" Hildy said. She is not really scientific-

minded. But she sensed what was hurting me most.
"Listen to me," she said. And gave a little speech on
why she considered me superior to other men.

I forgot what ailed me. I turned to reach for her
—and yelped with pain.

Hildy said I must stay quiet and not worry about
a thing. One of my worries was that Helen couldn't
stay to look after us because she was going to an
N.A.A.C.P. dinner. "I'll bring you anything you
want," Hildy said.

All I wanted was the lady; I expressed this forci-
bly, in active verbs.

"I've never understood," Hildy said, "why women
are supposed to be the ones who insist on getting
married. Men are much more marriage-minded."

I said maybe that was true in her experience. I
said it gloomily.

Hildy moved out of reach and said affectionate
things. Then she went to the kitchen.

Murmur of voices; women conferring on their invalid, his care and feeding. Helen's voice moved up
a notch: "He's really very healthy and strong. He
never even gets a cold."

"Yes, I know," Hildy said.

I heard Helen explain about what temperature to
set the oven to heat the French bread, and to bake
some frozen pastries. Murmur-mumble-mumble
again. Then Hildy's voice rising, ". . . after it burned

93

off his eyelashes I never used the oven again. Not that I'd ever used it myself, but guests would broil steaks . . ."

I wondered jealously whose eyelashes. I would do her a steak in the fireplace. I do very good steaks —shell sirloin over charcoal—why hadn't I thought of that sooner? While I could still get up and down?

". . . dial on HIGH till it boils," Helen was saying.

"Oh, I haven't seen a double-boiler in years," Hildy said. "I'd forgotten how sensible they are. Now tell me once more about the knobs. . . . HIGH is the other end from SIM. . . . I don't touch the BROIL knob because it's not BAKE . . ."

When Helen came in to say good night to me, she seemed apprehensive about leaving. She may have thought that this time it was the lady who would lose her eyelashes. She said the cats' food was already in their pans. "And if I wasn't on the committee for the N.A.A.C.P. dinner, I wouldn't rush off like this."

Hildy assured her we'd be fine.

I wasn't that sure. I had to lower myself downstairs as bumpety, if not as rapidly, as Pammy. And when I tried to lift logs for the fire I had to give up. "Damn it to hell."

The lady ordered me to sit. She brought logs— "Just little ones," I kept telling her anxiously—from the wood closet. She crumpled newspaper. And lit it. The newspaper burned beautifully. The wood only hissed. I knew it was probably still damp. And I knew just which log ought to be moved, so it wasn't too tight against the others. Fires have to breathe.

I instructed Hildy. We had often used the little fireplace in her apartment, even though in the city she paid three dollars a dozen for what I'd consider kindling size. I had always laid—or rearranged—the fire there while the lady watched. Now I watched. She moved the proper log as instructed. Flames started up.

She came and sat beside me. "After you began coming to see me," she said, "I wouldn't let anybody else build a fire there. While you were away in the winter, friends who came in the evenings would suggest having a fire. But I always said it was too warm in the room."

She said this looking at the fire, and as if it were not one of the most important things anybody had ever said.

It was quite a while before I thought about making drinks. Hildy had never made a Martini. In her apartment, guests mixed their own. She had once told me, "I never saw anybody make such a ritual of it as you do."

Sprained back or no, I was going to hold to the ritual. It is not a matter I entrust to amateurs.

"Tonight," Hildy said, "I am going to make your Martini." She was tenderly determined. Under the circumstances, no man could say No—or Huh?

Pammy came in from the kitchen where she'd

been eating, and tried to engage the lady by rubbing and rolling. "Not now, Pammy," the lady said. "I'm too busy."

I had never seen her so willing to take my advice. Even anxious. She consulted me like an acolyte, before filling a two-ounce measuring glass with gin. Clear to the brim, I told her; so full it bulges under surface tension. Very carefully, as one might while performing a laboratory experiment of the utmost delicacy, she poured from the brimming glass onto the ice in the mixer. Her hand was steady and nothing spilled; little lines formed between her brows as they do when she is concentrating. She said, "Now what?"

Pammy came over and looked up at me as if asking what now, indeed. She had never seen such goings-on in this house—a lady mixing drinks—and a lady she wanted freed for more worthy duties such as stroking a cat. She took out her feelings by mauling the only chair that was still relatively unscratched. I was too involved with being a back-seat bartender to yell at her.

We had come to the crucial step: the right amount of vermouth. A little less than a quarter of the measuring glass, I told Hildy. She held it out for me to see. Less, I told her. In using vermouth, I incline to the Mies van der Rohe theory of architectural adornment: Less is more.

"I think it would be easier to use an eyedropper,"

Hildy said. But she poured vermouth with great care, from the glass back into the bottle. I had never seen so much intentness in one slender back. "Do you think it's still a drop or two over?" she said, studying the result with lines of intentness in her delicate face.

I said I thought not. She added the exquisitely measured pale liquid to the gin in the mixer and stirred and stirred, which was right. My gin and vermouth live in the icebox and come out cold, as do the chilled glasses. So a little dilution is good.

"Oh, lord, I forgot the lemon." Self-reproach was vibrant in her voice.

When she sliced slivers of lemon peel, I was terrified she would cut herself. She didn't.

"You twist it," she said, when she brought me my drink. "Your fingers are stronger."

I twisted the lemon peel over the glass, and the oil flicked out and stayed in droplets on the top of the Martini. I rubbed peel around the edge of the glass while Hildy poured her sherry over ice. I turned and lifted the glass from the coffee table, and took the first sip. So help me, it was an excellent Martini. I told her so.

"But you made a face."

I said I'd turned too quickly and displeased my back. If I had made a face, it was a face about that.

But she went on watching me until she was sure. "I feel as if I'd invented the cure for rabies."

She forgot to serve grated Parmesan with the spaghetti; ordinarily I am rather particular about that, but I didn't remind her. She was too happy, too flushed with success and contact with an oven. "The next time," she said, "I think I'll put the French bread in sooner. But the spaghetti is really *hot*."

Afterward I watched her, through the open door to the kitchen, checking all the dials on the oven. "HIGH . . . two . . . three . . . four . . . five . . . six . . . SIM . . . OFF" she kept chanting to herself. ". . . off . . . Off . . . off . . . OFF. . . . I was relieved when she came back unscathed.

She said she hated having to leave the next day, that maybe she could figure out some way to stay three days longer and still get her notes in shape. I said, with noble insincerity, that I knew how much work was involved and she mustn't stint herself on the necessary time to prepare her talks. I waited for her to insist.

She said, How wonderful of me to be so generous-minded, so understanding—how different I was from other men.

Silently, I wished western Pennsylvania sunk to the bottom of whatever lake was big enough to hold it.

I wished I'd let the damn wheelbarrow drop and splinter to fragments.

Pammy kneaded her claws into my slacks in an

excess of sympathy or zeal. I told her to cut it out; I already had enough to contend with. She went upstairs; I heard a few muted thumps overhead, in my room, and guessed she had probably told Sherry it was safe to come down to the kitchen and eat, now that it was dark and empty.

My ears picked up the rattle of feeding pan on linoleum.

Hildy got up suddenly and started for the kitchen. I made a real effort to speak in a restrained tone: "Not now, dear. Sherry is eating. You'd scare her away."

Hildy froze into position. She whispered. "It's a bloody good thing you told me what happened to her in childhood. Otherwise I might get a trauma myself."

When the rattling died away, she muttered, "Now? I forgot to check the knob that did the bread."

"Not yet, dear," I said gently. "She's using her toilet pan."

It was several minutes before I heard the furtive padding on the stairs. I gave Hildy permission to move about freely. "And would you mind checking to see how much Sherry ate?"

Hildy came back again and reported. "There's one dollop of the gooey pink stuff left—about a tablespoonful—and a few of the little rocky things."

At least Sherry wasn't going on a hunger strike.

Hildy confessed she had left the oven on; it was

off now. I assured her it didn't matter. I told her for
perhaps the forty-ninth time that I didn't give a damn
whether she could cook.

Neither did Pammy. She finished off Sherry's dinner; then returned and settled on the lady, shedding
a largesse of hairs on Hildy's velveteen slack suit. It
was a smoky blue color that goes well with a fair-
skinned, blue-eyed lady. I thought how pretty she
looked—and all I could do was groan. And sit in a
rigid position.

I saw Pammy's ears go on the alert, and I saw her
glance up at the balcony. Sherry was there. She had
her head between the balusters and was looking
down at us. In the light from the foot of the stairs her
eyes were glaring red. I knew the technical reason—
Siamese were probably once albino—but I felt slightly
nervous anyway. It was like being chaperoned by a
panther.

Not that we needed a chaperone. Not with my
back.

The next morning Helen came in time to get
breakfast. That afternoon she drove Hildy into Ridgefield to take a bus for New York. She was gone longer
than I'd expected—the bus was late—and I had
worked myself into a bog of self-pity by the time she
came in.

Now that I had a good listener, I was loudly

mournful: "I couldn't have picked a worse time to sprain my back."

Helen looked at me thoughtfully. "Well, yes, you could. The first night she was here."

VI

Thunderclap

🐦🐦🐦

HILDY HAD GIVEN me a list of all the places she would
be, with phone numbers. She was taking a jet flight
to Pittsburgh first, then transferring to a small plane
that she said would "hop on up" to Franklin, Pennsylvania.

"'Hop' over the Allegheny Mountains?" I asked
in a stricken voice. I myself hadn't flown for thirty or
more years. I do not believe that men are meant to fly,
particularly over mountains in early spring.

Hildy assured me it was quite safe. "While my
parents were alive I was flying there two or three
times a year, and nothing ever happened."

That didn't reassure me. With my total distrust
of planes added to my native ability to worry, I knew
that now would be the time for a crash. The frail little
craft would never make it over the mountains. "Is it
a two-engine job?" I asked Hildy on the phone the
night before she left New York. We were talking several times a day.

"I never counted," she said. "All I know is that it has two wings."

I knew she had flown most of her life, and that she had once taken a flying lesson in a Piper Cub to write a magazine piece about it. She had told me a bit about that: "The instructor-pilot said to me, 'Now you do such-and-so, just the way you do when you're driving a car.' And I said, 'But I've never driven a car.' And he said, 'Good God.' I had a marvelous time with the joy stick once we got up in the air. You can make the plane tilt on its side and zoom up or down."

"Promise me you won't take over the controls," I said on the phone that night. "And you're to give the pilot of the little plane a message from me. Tell him he's carrying the most valuable cargo he will ever get. And tell the copilot too, in case the pilot gets a heart attack."

Hildy giggled. I felt she wasn't taking this desperate emergency nearly seriously enough.

I worried for two. I phoned her in Franklin exactly when she said she'd arrive. She was there. She said they'd had to wait over an hour and a half in Pittsburgh because of some engine trouble. "But I know how you are about planes, so I added two hours on when I gave you our time of arrival."

I told her how thankful I was she had come over the mountains safely. And I told her a great deal more I was thankful for. I said I still couldn't entirely believe it when she wasn't near me. . . . She said, "Of course I do. You ought to know that by now."

I said it was something I'd never expected to happen to me at my. . . . She knew what I was going to say. I had said it before, perhaps too often.

"Come off it," she said. "After all, we're only young twice."

My sprained back improved slowly; I still couldn't bend over to put on socks without moaning. Helen and the cats were sympathetic. Especially Helen. She stayed to fix dinners for the invalid, and we had one topic of conversation: Miss Dolson. Or rather, I had one topic and Helen humored me. But it was more than that.

Hildy had told me, "When the bus came, in Ridgefield, Helen and I flung our arms around each other and we almost cried."

Helen said, "I've been thinking maybe we should do the guest room over. It's not as pretty and bright as it ought to be for Miss Dolson. Why don't you ask her in a letter what ideas she has for changing it?"

Miss Dolson replied succinctly: "I wish you would take down those two drawings of kittens. They're so coy they make my stomach churn. And could you give me an ash tray for the bedside table that doesn't have a kitten on it? Beyond that, let's wait."

Wait for an occasional guest? Or for my lady to come home to stay?

Pammy, for one, was tired of waiting. She sat on the floor in front of me, the first evening we were alone, and looked at me with what seemed a question in her face: *What have you done with her?* I said, "It's all right, Pammy. The lady will come back."

Several times she seemed to hear something I didn't hear and turned head and set ears toward the floor above and listened—I had no doubt of that—for the tapping of heels on bare floor. She listened, too, as I did, for "da-ooma-guppa-ooma-da." She kept on listening for days, as I did. I kept telling her that the lady would come back, but her belief dwindled after a time. But now and then, for no reason I could understand, hope returned. She would suddenly go up the stairs and along the balcony to the guest-room door and sit in front of it and listen there. And she would sniff at the crack under the door, because to cats rooms smell of people who have been in them. The way people smell is important to a cat.

I told Hildy how Pammy felt, in a good many letters from upper Westchester County to western Pennsylvania, and how Pammy listened for the tapping of heels and a light voice singing. (Sherry's attitude was too evidently one of "well, that's over," but I didn't go into that.) Sherry began to come down from the balcony and, after cautiously looking around, settle with Pammy on their favorite chair.

She never sat on my lap if Pammy was around. Pammy had always been number-one cat. Pammy knew it—was confident of it. And Sherry knew it too. I always thought she said what Pammy told her to say, and did pretty much what Pammy wanted her to do. The only thing she had first call to—exclusive rights to—was the scratching post. Pammy wouldn't touch it; she preferred furniture.

If I came upon Sherry alone, and bent to stroke her, that deep, throbbing purr would begin. And she had been coming home every day at a decent hour, since the lady had left us.

I wrote Hildy about an essay on cats a retired sea captain had sent me. A very literate essay. I told Hildy, "But I've never encountered the time sense he thinks is in all cats. The only time sense mine have ever displayed was to be somewhere else when wanted." The cats weren't looking over my shoulder when I wrote that, and I wanted to amuse the lady.

Her schedule on the trip was rather exhausting, as such things always are. And at Allegheny College, on top of crowded days, she was reading students' manuscripts every night till late. "But out of thirty or forty I've come across two who may turn out to be real writers some day," she said, "so that's exciting." I didn't find it exciting at all. I didn't want her up there in western Pennsylvania discovering new young writers. I wanted her to come back and discover a writer named Lockridge.

I was phoning her every night, and I felt more

encouraged the night she said she couldn't keep from mentioning me constantly. "Not in classes, but every-where else. The word has gotten around." That after-noon she had been at a symposium where students were encouraged to ask questions about writing. "One girl got up and said, 'Miss Dolson, I have a ques-tion: How did you meet Richard Lockridge?'"

And one of the professors had asked her if she couldn't induce me to come to Allegheny with her the next time—"as a team."

That seemed a good time to remind her again it would simplify things if we were married. I had al-ready told her what I knew from experience—that there's a sureness, a special kind of depth in a good marriage. I had had that kind of marriage for many years. I didn't stress that part of it too much—Hildy approved of my having been happily married but she'd said, "You don't have to talk about it quite so often." Nothing could be unlived. But Hildy and I would start new, however we started. One phrase of hers kept being a kind of song in my mind: "We're only young twice."

"Would you object to being known as Mrs. Rich-ard Lockridge?" I wrote her. "I've never much liked the name Richard."

She said Richard was fine. "And I've never gone around with a Richard before. So that's all the nicer."

I didn't want her to go around with me—I

wanted her to stay put with me. She didn't promise that, but she did sound rather wifely, fussing about my health. I kept assuring her, with hollow heartiness, that I was "getting much better." And that I would feel all right as soon as she got back. I said bravely I was sure it was nothing malignant.

She sounded so anxious I became more and more cheerful. This wasn't like me; it made her more anxious. I must be keeping something from her. She couldn't bear to be away from me any longer. She was scheduled to leave that coming Saturday, five days later; she said she'd found she couldn't get an earlier reservation on a commercial plane because it was the week before Easter. "What is the nearest small airfield to you?"

"Danbury," popped out of my mouth.

"I'll cancel my last appointments," she said. "I'll charter a little plane with a pilot and fly in to Danbury tomorrow."

I was so elated at the thought of seeing her several days early that it took me at least ten seconds to react on "little plane—charter—Danbury."

I assured her hurriedly that there was no great emergency. My enthusiasm about the wonderful condition of my back mounted rather wildly, and apparently convinced her. She finally agreed to keep to her original schedule.

At least she would be coming down on a bigger airfield than Danbury—Kennedy or Newark or La

Guardia. They'd have ambulances waiting in case of a crash landing. And fire-fighting equipment.

On Saturday morning, as I studied the weather map in the *Times,* I had a new worry: a storm of considerable intensity showed on it and the storm seemed to be heading for western Pennsylvania. Probably flights would be canceled; surely they would be canceled. She would call from there and tell me that. Maybe I could even talk her into taking a train. It was stormy in the East; it must be even worse in western Pennsylvania.

I had made a little progress in my search for a story gimmick and went up to my office that morning at the usual time and got paper and pencil ready. I spent the morning waiting for the phone to ring—for a voice to tell me I could stop worrying because the flight was canceled. The phone didn't ring. The gimmick which had seemed possible the day before slipped meaninglessly through my mind. Now it wasn't just raining—it was thundering and lightning. Were the fly boys mad, to go up on this sort of day? A suicide squad?

Helen had planned to leave soon after lunch; her grandchildren were coming for the weekend and I was enough recovered to shift for myself. But the phone stayed maddeningly silent. And Helen stayed on, mercifully, probably figuring her grandchildren were in a better mental state than I was.

Around four o'clock I was drinking still another

cup of coffee when the phone blared. Helen started across the long room to answer it; I covered the distance in two or three leaps.

Hildy was safe; she had just landed at La Guardia. She would come up by train from New York the next morning. She had to get some things together—unpack and repack. The storm? Oh, yes, it had been rather bumpy. Nothing to worry anybody. Thunder and lightning? Oh, yes—beautiful, spectacular, to ride through the sky in all that.

I came back to finish my coffee. I seemed to have spilled most of it into the saucer when I took off.

Helen said, "I hadn't realized you were *that* worried."

I was to meet Hildy's train in New Canaan. I allowed enough time to drive the seven miles; I had only a little under an hour to wait.

Hildy had brought a good bit more luggage this time. The heaviest suitcase was mostly record albums, she said. "And I got us Ella Fitzgerald singing Gershwin—four sides."

My back was equal to the load.

Pammy was at the door. When she saw the luggage, she ran up the stairs—just a few steps—then came down to rub against the lady in an ecstasy of welcome.

Sherry, on the balcony, let out one furious, "Aow —naow" and vanished. I did not go after her.

And we never got to the third and fourth sides of Ella Fitzgerald that night. We were busy getting engaged. Hildy said, "No two people were ever better engaged."

She said she couldn't possibly get married before late summer. I protested it didn't make sense. She said, "Well, it would to a woman." I said I wasn't a woman. Hildy said, "Yes, darling, I'd noticed."

She didn't want an engagement ring. "I never wear rings." But she said she would love flowers as an engagement present. "I don't want them sent. I want to go to a greenhouse and go hog-wild."

We went to Pinchbeck's, on Peaceable Street, a day or so later. I'm not sure whether it was sunny that day; all I remember is Hildy walking radiantly along the paths in the greenhouse, between earth-filled tables, saying, "I'll take a dozen of those . . . and a dozen of these . . . and a dozen of that."

We had enough yellow and white flowers to fill our whole house.

Hildy said, "I didn't ask the price of anything. It must have cost you an awful packet. But at least it's cheaper than a diamond ring."

She and Helen dug out vases from cupboards. "I'm not sure we have enough," Hildy said. "But I'll start making a list of things we'd like for wedding presents. Then, when a relative or friend asks us what we need, I'll just tell them some item. But the only trouble is, how do we know how much they want to spend?"

I said we could solve that easily, by having several different lists. The first would be: Gifts We Want Under $5. . . . Then, Gifts We Want Between $10 and $20. . . . And last, Gifts if You Want to Shoot the Works and Money Is No Object, Hardly." Hildy said it was the most sensible idea she'd ever heard of, for weddings.

She spent a couple of hours arranging flowers. Pammy jumped to the kitchen counter and helped as only a cat can help; she battled stems and sniffed blossoms; she drank from a newly filled vase, her head framed in daffodils and laurel leaves. Hildy crooned, "You look like a Rousseau—a jungle cat." Pammy didn't seem to mind.

Whenever a bouquet was finished—beautifully finished—Pammy would rearrange it even if she had to stand on her hind legs with taller vases. Only when one is trying to wrap packages can a cat be of more help than when one is arranging flowers.

There were vases on every flat-topped surface in the living room except my bar. I had balked—I wouldn't even allow a bud vase there. A man must be firm about those things.

Pammy walked delicately over table tops making a last check to be sure every bouquet smelled right.

Then she came over and sat on the lady's lap and, with her indoor work done for the day, dozed off.

Hildy was looking around happily. "It's such a handsome big room. And it could take a lot of color."

I agreed that it could. I thought she meant flowers.

"Do you really like that painting over the stereo?" Hildy asked me. "We could bring one up from my apartment. And if we got new lampshades, and a slipcover. . . ." I must have looked rather taken aback; Hildy said she was sorry if she'd sounded bossy.

She hadn't. I told her that a room, too, can be young twice.

But when she asked if we could move the scratching post to some place less conspicuous, I said, "We'd have to see how Sherry reacts. She might not like it moved."

VII

Ripening

❧❧❧

I HAD ALREADY told the cats our news; I said I wanted them to be among the first to know.

Pammy purred. This may have been because I was stroking her at the time. Sherry stalked to the terrace door and demanded to get out. She went off with the air of a cat who was never coming back. She was back in time for lunch. Her attitude now was more, if you promise to keep that woman out of my sight . . .

Helen probably knew before we did. She hugged us and said, "You know what I wish you, but you already have it."

We called members of Hildy's scattered family and told them. They took it very well. I learned Hildy had given her sister and brother a first hint on airmail postcards which stated simply, "Never have I felt this way before in my whole life. I may even have to get married."

Now she told them, as she had told me, "Not before late summer." She said she didn't want to be a bride wrapped up in veils, so they mustn't bother coming long distances just for the wedding. We'd go to a justice of the peace and be married without any fuss.

That suited me fine. But waiting till late summer did not suit me in the least. When we asked Hildy's old friends the Epsteins if they'd be our witnesses— say, the end of August—I formed an instant bond with Sam because he said, "Sure . . . but why wait?"

Hildy, as I have mentioned, has a streak of Dutch stubbornness along with the Scotch-Irish. I am Scotch-Irish too, but I have enough Norwegian in me to counter her Dutch—plus a dash of French that sometimes gives me an edge. Whenever Hildy had to go into New York that spring, I arranged business matters so that I had to be in town too. I always drove her in and stayed at the hotel down the block. The walk to her apartment was fine when I was going the half block down Ninth Street. But the walk back to the hotel at 1 or 2 A.M. was endless. "My legs buckle," I told Hildy. "We ought to get married right now."

She was scared at the thought of moving out of New York so finally. Even the prospect of clearing out the apartment dismayed her. Not the physical labor; it was the ripping up of her whole past pattern as a loner. She told me she had stayed awake all one night worrying about it. As a worrier, Hildy can't touch me; she has no real talent for it. So I knew this was serious. We solved it together quite simply: we would keep her three-room apartment for our New York base, as long as we could afford it. Once that was settled, Hildy stopped feeling torn. Oddly, from then on, whenever we were in town, she always talked about "going home to the country."

She had been excited, when she came back from western Pennsylvania, over the change in the countryside after two weeks of spring. She had said exultantly, "The green is rushing."

Forsythia was already spilling gold. When sun hit the budding maples in late afternoon, we watched a pale bronze radiance reach to the sky. Soon apple and cherry trees frothed into blossom, even the gnarled old tree by the driveway. Lilac bushes were so heavy-laden they flowed in a sea of color. Hyacinths ringed the pear tree like a Maypole. What I think are bayberry bushes flowered with tiny white bells. Oriental poppies flamed near the bridal wreath bush. Nature was all on my side.

We were married late in May, that spring of our second youth.

Not by a justice of the peace; somehow that hadn't seemed right. We had driven around the countryside looking for a church we liked, confident that a clergyman would go with it. The church we found was old and lovely; it stood, white and gracious, on a rise in South Salem, which is the hamlet nearest the house and the one from which mail comes. I fumbled a little when I was putting a ring on a finger which had never worn a ring before. I almost broke up on one of the responses and afterward I told Helen that. She said, "Yes, I thought you did. But your voice certainly came out good and strong on 'I do.' I never heard you sound firmer." Helen was one of a handful of friends at the wedding.

It didn't occur to either Hildy or me to send an announcement to any newspaper, specifically, the *Times*. We didn't think they'd care. Our friend Mildred Wohlforth, another wedding guest, asked us tactfully a week or two later if we'd mind if she wrote a little story about our wedding for the Ridgefield *Press*. "People around here keep asking me if you're married. They're very interested."

They could have looked at my wife's fourth finger left hand, but that wouldn't always have worked. Hildy kept sliding the ring off because she said it made her feel as if she'd caught her finger in a knot-hole. Sometimes she forgot and left it on a dressing table. Helen, when she did our bedroom, would bring it down and hand it over stealthily, like a hot jewel slipped to a fence, smiling at both of us.

Hildy had heard about a cat that loved jewelry, and she asked me anxiously if either of our cats was addicted that way and might swallow the ring accidentally. I wasn't sure whether she was more concerned about the ring or the cats. I told her our cats wouldn't touch the stuff. Privately, I suspected that Sherry, if the opportunity rose, would drop the ring down a drain.

Sherry still refused to come in from outside if Hildy was in sight. During the first weeks of our marriage, the portals rang with my rallying cry, "Get back! Don't let Sherry see you."

Hildy took it quite amiably, although being treated as a new kind of scare-cat couldn't have been pleasant.

Pammy was more ardent than ever, now that we had our lady full time. And gaily determined in whatever she did, including wooing. After I put up the screen doors, Pammy, if nobody came to let her in, would leap against the screen midway up and hang on, clawing impatiently. When Hildy tried to read the paper, Pammy would fling herself against the *Times* like a clown through a paper hoop. Even when she was a nuisance, she was so charming we couldn't resist her.

Hildy began to worry about the effect of this on Sherry. Whenever she could get within ten feet of Sherry, she would croon something reassuring: "Darling, you mustn't feel rejected. . . . Your wicked stepmother wants to love you. . . . You mustn't be afraid, sweet cat."

Sherry was so terrified, or nervous, that her muscles would twitch convulsively. Hildy didn't try to

touch her—that would have sent Sherry into a panic—
she just went on talking sweetly. "I'm using child psy-
chology on her, I think."

In answer, Sherry would let out a hideous yowl—
"a-ow—a-ow"—that sounded hostile to ears unaccustomed to Siamese talk, or to any hostile talk, for that
matter. Hildy was not used to being disliked.

At night when we went up to the big bedroom
where our cats were having a late-evening snooze, she
would say, "I'll go in first and that will clear the room
faster."

But the signal had already gone out, to pointed
cat ears: two people coming upstairs. Meaning:
"Scram." By the time we went into the room, there
was no cat in sight. With Pammy, it was more than
ever a game; sometimes she would wait just long
enough to let us see her dive under a bed. After that,
it was a matter of hand-and-knee groping. Once,
when Hildy and I were crawling beside the bed
shielding Pammy, I remembered a story about our
Ridgefield vet, Dr. Dann, who had given us Pammy.
He was just starting off on vacation when his own
two cats went under a bed, and it took him so long to
flush them out he was two hours late getting away.

This struck Hildy as so funny she rolled on the
floor laughing. We both laughed so hard that Pammy
got offended and emerged of her own accord.

We developed another, better, system of flushing

Pammy from under the bed. One of the heavy cushions from the office couch could be shoved far enough under to be a cat propellant. Usually, of course, Pammy managed to dodge under the other bed. She enjoyed it all very much.

With Sherry, it was no longer a game. She still hid, but more out of animal terror. The minute I flushed her out, she would give a wild look at the lady and make a desperate race for the open door to the hall.

One night Sherry wasn't in the bedroom. We got Pammy out with no more than the usual trouble, but Sherry had vanished utterly. Not behind the curtain, not under beds, chair, or the sofa that had been moved from downstairs to replace the one that had been moved down from upstairs. Hildy and I searched the entire room, even the closets. I was convinced I had heard two cats overhead, so I looked to see if Sherry had wedged herself under the convectors that heat the second floor. There was no possible place the cat could be.

Maybe she had somehow dodged past us? We closed off the bedroom so that Pammy couldn't get back in. Then Hildy searched the rest of the upstairs while I covered the downstairs. No Sherry. I checked all the doors: closed. So was the one window that had been left unscreened because sometimes cats preferred to enter there, up the pear tree and over the roof.

Sherry couldn't have got out, I kept telling myself fearfully. I was coming back along the upstairs hall just as Hildy opened the door of the room we had, in effect, sealed off after the search. There sat Sherry in the middle of the room, washing up. Having sent the humans off on a wild-goose chase, she had been feeling too smug in victory to hear us come back. She hunched her shoulders and ran so fast her back legs caught up with her front, as she detoured the lady and escaped.

We never found out where she had been. There was no place she could have been. Cats are good at that sort of thing. They dematerialize at will.

Any cat owner accepts that, but Hildy didn't, quite. She would say, "Do you think Sherry could have been hanging like a bat behind a picture?"

I let her try to solve that mystery alone; I was working on a new mystery novel. Hildy hadn't yet gone back to work on her novel. She wrote in a magazine piece later, "I was too busy being a wife and making out lists and peering thoughtfully into the freezer."

The freezer was well-stocked, thanks to Helen. And there were silver-foiled bundles of fresh asparagus that Hildy and I were cutting every day; Helen froze whatever we couldn't use right away. Mr. Salvestrini had recovered from cat wounds enough to clean the bed in mid-April. Hildy inquired solicitously about his arm, when they met. Mr. Salvestrini seemed moved that she remembered. He said, "It was a cat I'd known for years and all of a sudden it just turned on me. . . ." He imitated a savage beast clawing, biting. He showed Hildy his scar. Afterward I told my wife, just as an antidote, something a doctor had told me: "Cat bites aren't good, but they're better than people bites. Cleaner." I did not repeat this to Mr. Salvestrini; he did a fine job on the asparagus bed.

The first day my bride and I went out with long knives to cut, she acted as if I'd led her to buried treasure, and exclaimed over each stalk. When we brought the colander of asparagus to the kitchen sink, I told her the stems always had to be scraped, before cooking.

"No," Hildy said. "We're not going to scrape. I refuse to waste our time in any such fussy operations."

That was her over-all attitude: "Ten minutes at a stretch in a kitchen is enough." I found I enjoyed this casual approach, especially since I preferred not to have her out of my sight any longer than necessary. In her own absent-minded way, she was quick, deft and orderly. And except on such matters as scraping asparagus, she asked my advice and praised my expertise. I was Oven-Eye and Meat Department. She told a friend, "Dick always knows when to poke something or take it off." We ate well, although the time of our evening meal was somewhat erratic.

I gained ten needed pounds. So did my ninety-five-pound wife. And she decided suddenly that from now on she would get up early ("Early" was eight-fifteen) to fix our breakfast.

Pammy and Sherry had been used to waiting for me on the landing every morning. As soon as I came out of the bedroom, they accompanied me down to the kitchen and the first order of business: their breakfast. The lady would drift down about an hour later.

The day of her debut as early-riser, the cats were waiting on the landing as usual; when they saw Hildy instead of me, they couldn't believe their eyes. Hildy told me later, "Even Pammy was stunned. And Sherry reared back in horror, projecting 'Not you! Surely not you, O wicked stepmother. What foul trick is this?'"

Pammy recovered very quickly and bounded up on the back counter to help Hildy open the jar of junior beef. Sherry refused for weeks to eat a breakfast prepared by the lady until the lady was safely away from the kitchen. Gradually, Sherry cut down the quarantine period; she would go into the kitchen after a minute or two, and watch from a cautious distance as Hildy spooned out food for cats.

As a usual thing, each cat got half the contents of a freshly opened jar. But occasionally one cat would skip a meal so that there'd be a half jar left over. One morning, for some reason, Sherry arrived in the kitchen even before Pammy. Hildy had found a half-open jar that had sat out overnight in warm weather; the meat is thoroughly cooked, but Hildy was a little doubtful. She scooped a tiny amount up with a spoon to taste, because, she said later, "I thought if anybody was going to get botulism it had better be me—I'm bigger."

Sherry took one look at the lady eating a cat's breakfast, and let out so furious, ear-ripping a scream I came down half-dressed to see what had happened. Sherry was still screaming her rage. Hildy said, "Sherry always suspected I was a fiend, and this proved it. I've set the cause of stepmothers back about two hundred years." It did take Sherry some little time to recover from this ghastly experience.

The cats had been trained never to come into the dining room to beg while humans were eating. Hildy admired their discipline; she said that at home all the children had sneaked food to dogs under the table. The only time our cats broke the rules, even partway, was when we had lamb or chicken, and they'd go swirling round and round the table and under it. It did them no good. They would then withdraw to the living room and Pammy would brief Sherry: "Speak up. Make a real stink." Sherry enjoyed voicing their grievances.

The first time Hildy cut up some leftover bits of chicken and put it in their pans after dinner, she said happily, "They'll have a surprise midnight snack." At the time—around nine—both cats were upstairs napping. Within five minutes they had come down to gobble the treat.

What puzzled Hildy, who was used to dogs, was that our cats never showed the slightest interest when we had beef for dinner. I pointed out that after all, they ate junior beef three times a day, so that their attitude was rather, ho-hum, not beef *again*.

They weren't allowed to get up *on* anything in living room or dining room to snitch food. This was perfectly understood. Once we had guests for cocktails, with shrimps for hors d'oeuvres. Pammy came in and greeted the guests nicely. Then she retired under a coffee table. I was busy making drinks, and it was a while before I saw a paw reach up delicately and hook a shrimp from an hors d'oeuvres plate. It vanished under the table; then another, and another. Technically, she was within the rules. One can't expect too much of cats.

But I was prepared to raise hell with Pammy if she clawed the new slipcover Hildy was having made for a living-room sofa.

This was the sofa that had been up in the big

bedroom. We had changed so many things around, Helen said, "Every morning, when I come in, I look forward to seeing what's different from the night before." Hildy had complained that everything in the living room was "leggy," so it had been my idea to shift sofas: a leggy one up, a skirted one down. The only drawback was that both sofas weighed roughly as much as an elephant. Helen said she would enlist her nephew's help, and he could bring along one or two friends, as soon as he came back from vacation. Hildy and I drove into the village on errands; when we came home we gaped in astonishment: there sat the upstairs couch downstairs. Helen said, "I just slung them over my shoulder." What had happened was that the milkman and the cleaner's delivery van had arrived in the driveway at the same time. Helen had appealed to them wistfully: did they know anyone who would do this little job? They had responded with instant gallantry, and considerable heaving of muscles. When Hildy tried to express our thanks to the milkman later, he said, "But we weren't doing it for *money*. We did it for Mrs. Holmes."

The one thing Helen couldn't do was persuade cats not to claw. And both Helen and I were a bit anxious about Hildy's reaction if she saw a new slipcover ripped to tatters. Helen had once said to Hildy, "You have to realize that cat people never really see the damage cats do." And Hildy had said, "Well, I see it."

The slipcover man arrived in late morning while both cats were out. I heard the women ooh-ahing so delightedly I knocked off work early, to join the home-decorating group. Hildy and I had picked out the fabric: a white English linen strewn with yellow flowers and green leaves. It looked lovely in the front corner flanked by windows. As I admired it, I took frequent peeks out a window, waiting for disaster to arrive on eight feet.

Pammy came home first. She was so intent on examining the new possession she hardly stopped to roll over at Hildy's feet. She sniffed the pleated skirt; she walked around the sofa thoughtfully three or four times; suddenly she jumped up on the seat and settled on a fat cushion, paws tucked under her, riding boat-fashion. She purred.

For the rest of that week, both cats sat on that sofa so constantly we humans almost never got a chance. They sat side by side, reverent as cats in church, looking quite exalted and purring in soft-pedal organ tones. It was the first time Sherry had sat in a room with us since Hildy came. I have never quite understood it. A friend suggested that the linen was too smooth for Pammy to get her claws into properly, but that is nonsense. To a cat, the only impervious covering is sheet metal. I think perhaps the real explanation is that Pammy said to Sherry, "Look, the lady has fixed this up charmingly for us. Let's show our appreciation."

Sherry, after the first incredulous look at her scratching post in its crazy new position, had resigned herself to using it whenever the mood came over her. Pammy still clawed other furniture occasionally, to keep her hand in, but she didn't touch the lady's pretty slipcover.

There was one period when I was afraid she'd attack it for revenge, after the quarrel.

VIII

Quarrel

No HUMAN KNOWS what goes on in a cat's mind, which is sometimes probably as well. But one can accept behavior as evidence. Pammy, that summer, behaved like a cat who had fallen in love. She followed Hildy everywhere she could. When Hildy stopped walking, Pammy rolled over at her feet. Sometimes she did this when Hildy had not stopped walking, with that curious confidence most cats have—a confidence often misplaced—that they will not be stepped on. It was this need to be close that led to the quarrel.

Hildy went to a terrace door one morning to see how many new iris had come out overnight. She wore a robe over a nightgown and it was a chilly morning; she changed her mind about going out. Pammy had followed to the door, planning to go out too. When Hildy stopped abruptly, her robe swirled and brushed the attendant cat.

She did not really bump Pammy and certainly did not step on Pammy. But Pammy let out the howl of a cat undergoing torture. She leaped away, crouched, flattened her ears. She glared at Hildy and I thought for a moment she was going to hiss at her. She did not go that far.

"I couldn't have hurt her," Hildy said. "I know I didn't. I didn't step on her." She moved toward Pammy, talking to her, saying how sorry she was, then kneeling down with her arms out. Pammy leaped away and ran partway up the staircase.

It was evident from her movements that no paw had been stepped on and she did not stop to lick her tail, as she would have done—ostentatiously—if her tail had been trodden. It was, obviously, her feelings which had been hurt. She had not been damaged; she had been betrayed. Her beloved had made a false move.

Oddly, since cats for the most part forgive quickly, Pammy for more than two days ran whenever Hildy came near her. She would not let Hildy touch her nor sit on Hildy's lap, however cordial the invitation. What was more, she would not sit on my lap either, when Hildy and I sat side by side, as we usually did. I, by association, was also guilty of this unforgivable affront. She clawed the furniture in furious spurts. Several times she approached the new slipcover, then looked back at the lady with a *Just you wait* air. But mostly she wouldn't even look at Hildy.

By the third day, I had had enough of it. I picked Pammy up, although she squirmed a little.

"That's enough of that," I told our cat. "Come off it, Pammy. You hear me? Come off it."

I spoke sternly and put the cat down on the floor.

Pammy looked up at me for a moment and then went across the room and rubbed against Hildy's ankles. When Hildy reached down to stroke her, Pammy rolled over on the floor, purring.

It was largely chance, of course, and I told my wife that. If one instructs a cat to do what the cat was about to do anyway, amazing results may be achieved. Hildy accepted my explanation, but only, I think, in part.

Another time, Sherry came in from the kitchen with something on her nose.

"Wash your face, Sherry," I said, using the same tone of command I had used when I told Pammy to come off it. Sherry immediately sat down and washed her face. Hildy stared at me. She may have wondered, for that instant, what she had got herself into. Witches and cats have long been familiars; she may have wondered if wizards shared in this historically sinister relationship.

It was about this same time—midsummer—that Hildy and I had our one serious quarrel. My wife was deeply hurt and angry; I said that what I had done was incredibly stupid and thoughtless. Hildy said, Yes, it most certainly was. I felt one apology was enough; I became very clipped and cool. Hildy said, "Don't be so bloody British." And went out for a walk.

Whatever wizard powers I had over cats didn't work on the lady. It was midnight before she calmed down; the storm's backlash took several days to die out.

I knew things were all right when I heard her singing again. It was a sound I always listened for—that and her quick footsteps. And all the more now that she had gone back to work on her novel. I had suggested she take over the upstairs guest room as an office. Helen's nephew moved the twin beds from there to the guest room downstairs, and replaced them with the double bed. Hildy writes propped up against pillows, in longhand on a clipboard, so she needed a big bed as an office. She had been in the habit of working all day, but now she wanted to fit to my schedule: as an ex-newspaperman, trained first on the rewrite desk, I turn out four, five, or six typed pages in a morning and that's my stint for the day. Hildy's pace is considerably slower, but she had offered to knock off when I did, soon after noon, and join me for a pre-lunch drink. The only minor flaw in this plan was that when Hildy was working well, she forgot she had a husband. If she ran on till long after one o'clock, Pammy and I would sit together, listening for the sounds of our lady. But a lady lying on a big bed writing with soft-lead pencil can be very silent. I would drop a small hint finally, by yelling, "The cats and I are desolate. . . . The cats and I crave companionship."

I used *cats* in the plural out of courtesy. Sherry still preferred a room empty of the lady. She had begun to make the best of the situation, but always implying that the best was not very good.

Once Hildy went out to cut iris and surprised Sherry asleep in a dense clump of stalks, on cool earth. Sherry let out a bitter wail—do you have to track me down even here?—and bolted.

Pammy liked to help us in the garden, but she preferred a flirty game of hide-and-seek. Or she would dash up the ash tree and leap from branch to branch with a cat's precise targetry.

I didn't want to take a chance on seeds in the garden, because a freshly seeded bed is a temptation no cat tries to resist. And seeds are too slow for a lady who expects instant flowering miracles. We planted gladiolus bulbs instead, and marigold and zinnia plants. I had always thought of weeding flower beds as woman's work, but Hildy said it would bore her unless I were there too. To goad her, I quoted, "If one loves flowers, one must hate weeds more." My wife said what a dreary little motto. Eventually we weeded together; by the time we got around to the glads, we were weeding the weeds. But the glads were magnificent anyway, blooming gigantically the month after iris and rambler roses, after mock orange and laurel. The zinnias and marigolds looked fine—leafing, budding—till the day we went out and found the marigold stalks all bare, as leafless as pencil leads. I thought it was a blight of some kind, but I was afraid to use any strong spray because cats may lick leaves, or brush against a plant and then lick themselves. Hildy agreed we shouldn't take a chance; better a blight than a poisoned cat. Then, one dusk when we were setting up a croquet set on the lawn beyond the flower beds, we saw the blight. He had very long ears and a twitchy nose, and no fear of us at all. He sat so close, watching us at croquet, it appeared he was quite willing to substitute for a wicket. Our most threatening gestures resulted only in a few desultory hops.

Hildy muttered, "Who ever said 'timid as a rabbit'?" She was so indignant about our marigolds she asked me why our cats didn't go after rabbits. I told her that sometimes they did. "One time Martini found a nest of baby rabbits. By the time I could get out there, she had killed the whole lot. I never heard such horrible screams of agony."

Hildy looked stricken. "I just meant full-grown rabbits."

I told Pammy and Sherry, "Before you chase a rabbit, ask how old it is."

Perhaps our cats did chase the marigold gobbler; at any rate, he vanished, and our marigolds started bravely all over again and bloomed late and lavishly.

Our house was always full of flowers—our own.

We brought up several paintings from the apartment, and had two-handed games of "Let's just see how it would look over there." Once Sherry came in after what I gathered was a hard morning's hunting, and started upstairs to rest. Halfway up, she stopped dead, to look at a painting we had changed in her absence. She looked at it long and thoughtfully. My wife said, "I'd love to know what she thinks of it."

Now that Sherry was in viewing range for longer and longer periods, Hildy decided that much as she loved Pammy, our long, lean cat was the more classically beautiful of the two. "She could have been carved by ancient Egyptians." The one-sided chats with Sherry took on a strong tinge of aesthetics: Hildy would croon, "You have a noble set to your head. . . . Your body is all pure line. . . . You're a beautiful, beautiful creature. . . ." Sherry still screeched, "A-ow —a-ow," in answer, but it seemed to me she was beginning to listen.

I was talking about cats more than ever to Hildy, but now she asked for it—and listened. I made the mistake, early on in these general information sessions, of telling her that cats are only faithful to a mate the first few days. My wife was shocked. "But they're supposed to be so domestic." I said, Well, anyway, cats were intensely passionate for those few days, making love constantly. Hildy said darkly, "That makes it all the worse."

I told her I thought all cats were totally self-centered. "They think the world revolves around them."

"Even the neglected ones—the strays?"

I said, "The world still revolves around them, but in an angry blur."

Once she asked me what a cat used its whiskers for. I said the original theory was, to measure the width of an opening. "If its whiskers could get through a hole, then its body could follow. But of course that's nonsense." I said I hadn't the foggiest notion of what a cat's whiskers were really for.

I talked mostly about Siamese because that was the breed I knew best. "One reason Pammy is not a show cat is that when you lay her tail along her spine, it's supposed to reach to her shoulder blades—Sherry's does, but Pammy falls short."

My wife pointed out, with fierce inconsistency, that Pammy always carried her tail high—her "resolute" tail—and Sherry's tail hung down droopily. She was just as fierce in defending dogs. Now that we were safely married, I was apt to tease her about "man's dumb friend." I said tests showed they weren't nearly as bright as cats. My wife brushed this aside as "mere statistics." I said it was their personality I objected to more than any lack of brains. "They're backslappers, Rotarians, too waggish and hearty and anxious to please." I read her a passage on the difference between dog lovers and cat lovers from John Moore's

Waters Under the Earth: "A dogman loves having tails wagged at him; he likes being looked up to. He tends to be quite a good leader for that reason. Your catman, on the other hand, is always made a bit uncomfortable by those spaniel eyes and devoted tail-thumps on the floor."

Hildy said it was obvious I had never known any dogs of spirit.

I said I had had several dogs as a child, but I'd always liked cats better. I told her about the first cat I had, when I was seven, and how, when she died, my father and I buried her under a rosebush.

Hildy and I told each other a great deal about our childhoods, as lovers do when they are greedy to know every smallest part of the whole. We were surprised how many things were alike in our growing up, although we'd grown up in such different places physically—I in Kansas City, Missouri, and Hildy in Franklin, Pennsylvania. "Yes, dinner at six on the nose," one of us would murmur. . . . "Yes, we played that same game but we didn't call it Statues—we called it Still Waters No More Moving."

Our mothers had both loved Dickens. Mine had read Dickens aloud to me, a dozen volumes set in six-point type, two columns to a page. Hildy's mother had urged her oldest child to put aside the Rover Boys for Dickens, but, with three younger children, she hadn't had time to inject a dose word by word.

"But she read us the *Jungle Books,*" Hildy said, "and the 'Jabberwocky' and Kingsley's *Water Babies,* and a lot of other things. . . . Tell me again about how you hunted crawdads in the West Bottoms in Kansas City."

Her father and brothers had been keen on hunting and fishing, but western Pennsylvania evidently had no crawdads, so far as Hildy knew. I told her about the time I got a BB gun for my ninth birthday, and aimed it first thing at a bird on a branch in our backyard. To my horror and surprise, I hit the bird and killed it. I could still remember how devastated I'd been. I told my wife, "In grade school, I was taught to pronounce it de-*vass*-tate."

Hildy said she thought that was a much better pronunciation. "It sounds the way devastate feels."

We adopted "I was de-*vass*-tated" for our new collection of private jokes. And we would amuse each other by quoting, on unsuitable occasions, a line from Robert Graves: "It was all very tidy."

I often read poetry to Hildy, and Graves was one of our new favorites. We thought his *Frightened Men* was the best poem about cats—the interior nature of cats—we had ever known. I read a lot of Robert Frost too; as Hildy pointed out triumphantly, Frost was a dog lover. I liked him in spite of that.

Sometimes we had an overhead sound effect of cats while I read. Pammy had relaxed her monopoly;

if she had the lady's lap at breakfast, and before lunch and dinner, she allowed me almost exclusive rights in the evenings. By midsummer, both cats had relaxed enough to play the game of pursuit and mimic combat which is the big game of cats. Sherry still wouldn't relax that much in the lady's presence, so they played it upstairs of evenings. From above us there would be a wild rushing of feet which resembled more the pounding hooves of a herd of horses than the whisper of cats' padded paws.

It usually started in the big bedroom when one of them got bored with sleeping, decided it was time to play, and jumped the other. Sherry was more likely to be original aggressor, but, I think, in a way a child gets a parent to play. With things started, they would chase each other madly through the long hall which connected bedroom with office, usually reversing on the couch, but now and then, less acceptably, on my desk, where they had a tendency to skid on papers. One would chase the other back into the bedroom, and then the thumping began. I had watched them enough in the past to know that Pammy was usually the "up" cat, and Sherry the one who lay on her side and fended. It was just that Sherry was more loudly vocal about it; she would begin to make, by intention, the blood-curdling yowls of a cat who is about to take another cat apart and strew it widely.

At first, Hildy thought they were fighting; I told

her about the game, and assured her it was all pre-
tend, and great fun for cats.

One night I was reading T. S. Eliot's *Old Pos-
sum's Book of Practical Cats* to Hildy. I was in the
midst of "Growl Tiger," that delightful verse narra-
tive, reading with mounting beat as the warring Siamese approached, in sampans, the houseboat where
Growl Tiger was deep in dalliance with the Lady
Grittlebone. The Siamese were boarding, armed with
toasting forks, when we heard a wild scramble in the
hall above and then on the landing.

Both cats tumbled down the staircase, apparently locked together, and both were yelling and
snarling. They came to all fours at the bottom of the
stairs and faced each other and screamed. The tails
of both bristled to unlikely size and the fur stood up
along their backs. I thought our cats had simultane-
ously gone crazy.

But then, together, they swirled around and
faced the door, tails bushed and Siamese voices
threatening.

There was a cat outside looking in—a harmless
enough cat, so far as humans could tell. He looked in,
with no apparent animus and certainly with no tail
bushing. Our cats, who were quite used to seeing
other cats on the other sides of doors, slowly sub-
sided. The out-of-door cat stretched and indifferently
walked away.

I had never seen our two act so before. I suppose they had been aroused from sleep by some insulting remark the cat outside had made in passing and had raged down to take care of things.

Another time, it was not the cats that went crazy; it was I, or at least that's how it looked to my wife. We were standing at a front window watching some newly arrived swallows, admiring their graceful, gliding swoops. They were swooping back and forth across the driveway, close to the garage. Suddenly I let out a yell and charged out and slammed the garage door down in their faces. Just in time, too. "Barn swallows," I told my bewildered wife. "They'd decided to nest in the garage because it's the closest thing here to a barn. And once they nest and lay eggs, we can't drive the car in or out—it upsets them." I had been through that situation before. For several days, I kept the garage shut up tight, except when our cats were doing their patrol.

The frustrated swallows finally swooped off to nest someplace more hospitable. Helen kept us alerted on other arrivals; she identified the beautiful bird with shocking pink front as a scarlet tanager. None of us had ever seen one before, and when a second scarlet tanager came, we bragged all over Westchester and Fairfield Counties about our exotic pair. Helen pointed out another newcomer while we were having lunch. That was Hildy's and my best bird-looking time because the back wall of the dining room is mostly glass, overlooking the feeders. (The feeders are hung from slender branches that won't hold a cat's weight.) Helen pointed to her find on a branch of the nearest maple: yellow-orange head and front, with black; very handsome, very Halloweenish. She said she hadn't been able to locate one like him in her bird book.

"Look under Oriole," I said in an authoritative tone. Both women looked at me in astonishment. I was rather astonished myself. Helen riffled pages and reported, with suitable awe, "It's a hooded oriole."

When a new kind of yellow-orange and black combination arrived the next day, the women looked at me expectantly. After all, I had practically invented orioles in this household. I examined color plates in Helen's book and said I thought Baltimore oriole was the closest. "But he may be a differently marked hood." Now that I was leading ornithologist, I didn't intend to stick my beak out. The women weren't satisfied. Helen said, "I wish we could see him closer."

The oriole arranged that with tragic speed. Within minutes, there was a frightful thud against a window. Hildy and I ran out; there lay a bird on the grass, motionless. "Dead," I said. I felt all the sorrier because it was unmistakably a Baltimore oriole. And so lifeless I thought we should put him in a refuse can before our cats came home. But then he stirred faintly; Hildy said, "Let's put him in an open basket someplace up high and see if the air revives him." Helen joined the rescue squad. We dumped bulbs from baskets, chose the best one as bed or bier, lined it with leaves, and laid the bird in it. Hildy bent over the basket anxiously; the victim came to life and blasted her with angry cheeps. My wife jumped; it was rather like having a corpse talk back. Sherry appeared out of nowhere to investigate why all the humans were crouching on a woodpile. When we tried to corner her to put her inside, she whizzed off toward the back meadow. Our invalid lifted its brilliant Halloween head, cheeped louder, and flew to the nearest bush. But then it seemed to collapse. It sat slumped in a thicket of leaves, not stirring. Even my uphill optimist Hildy admitted after ten or fifteen minutes that things looked bad. What with keeping the deathwatch and watching out for cats, we were in quite an emotional state. Helen had gone back upstairs and was doubling as lookout. She called, "Pammy's coming over the back wall." Hildy and I moved fast, to the bush. The oriole, seeing us close in, gave a furious cry—almost Siamese-strident. It flapped to a higher twig; then it took off slowly, creakily, testing its invalid strength. My wife and I could hardly breathe, for hoping. The oriole soared up, up, up, strong and sure. We let out a shout of joy. Pammy thought we were welcoming her and trotted even faster.

One mark of the difference between our cats was the way they came over the wall when Hildy and I were in view. Pammy would rush straight across the lawn to us. Sherry would skulk along the wall, using every bush for cover, evading, cringing fearfully sideways, till she could get out of sight of the humans. But now that she would at least sit in the living room with us sometimes, Helen told my wife about the brush. When Helen and her husband had stayed in the house all winter, Mr. Holmes had brought out a scrub brush and somehow persuaded Sherry to submit to grooming. *Submit* wasn't the right word for long: Sherry, that fearful, skittish cat, had lapped up this special attention. "Pammy wouldn't stay still— she hated the whole operation," Helen said. "But Sherry would sit and purr under the brush for as long as an hour."

I had never done much cat-brushing, especially with a long-handled, coarse-bristled scrub brush. But I finagled Sherry onto my lap, alone; then my wife approached with the brush and tried, very gently, to stroke our cat's back. Sherry twitched and whimpered, then scrambled off my lap and ran across the room. Pammy, who had always scorned a brushing, instantly wanted this delicious attention from the lady. She sat on Hildy purring smugly as the brush went back and forth—against the fur, then smoothing that silken coat. During the entire time, Sherry sat stonily silent across the room, watching.

Whenever Hildy and I came home after an evening out, Pammy would hear the car, no matter how late or how fast asleep she had been, and come hurrying bumpety down the stairs to greet us and roll at Hildy's feet. There was always the ecstatic reunion—lady and cat. One cat. Sherry never came farther than the landing.

My wife grieved over it, mostly for Sherry's sake. Once, walking in the hummocky, often-swampy back woods, Hildy told me, she glimpsed, from a distance, what she thought was a wild animal, leaping with incredible grace, incredible lengths, from hummock to hummock. "Then I realized it was Sherry," Hildy said. "It was touching to see her that way—so free and unafraid."

Soon afterwards we saw Sherry in action much closer to home. We were eating lunch and muttering to each other about the low class of customers at the bird feeders. "Six pigeons," my wife said. "They've started coming in waddle-back lots."

The six went into a sudden noisy flap. Sherry, crouched behind a forsythia bush, emerged in full leap. Helen said afterward, "As if she were flying through the air cross-legged." The pigeons barely got off the ground as Sherry landed. Hildy said, "Cat among the pigeons! Now I see what it means."

Once my wife called me breathlessly to come and

look at "an exotic new bird. It has a dark background and an overlay of shimmering colors." It turned out to be a starling. And it did shimmer with color in the sunlight.

Hildy wanted me to teach her about wind shifts. "How do you tell from watching the leaves?" I said I picked trees a little distance away, because there were too many eddies close to our house to be a true indication. I started to tell her what it meant when the wind shifted from south to northeast, but then I discovered she didn't even know where north was. I finally drew a large compass on the terrace flagstones and painted it bright green. Hildy said, "This is the first time I've ever known where I was." She would study it carefully before she went roaming off to collect all sorts of wild blooming things to use in bouquets. When she brought in some "pretty lacy white stuff" she thought might be Queen Anne's lace, she was sneezing so hard she could hardly talk. "It's ragweed," I said. Even then she could hardly bear to throw the stuff out, although in hay fever season, especially, she's allergic to all such nose ticklers.

She asked me suddenly, "What would you have done if I'd been allergic to cats?"

I said, "I'd have given away the cats."

"Oh," she said, in a small voice. As if it were the first time she had realized the depth of my feeling for her.

By late summer, as the days grew smaller, twi-
lights had a special golden haze. Pammy and Sherry
sat inside a screen door, one such twilight, sniffing
the air. They were so silent about it, and so yearning,
I felt a bit mean about not letting them out for another run. Pammy had already had one contraband
outing that week. On a very hot day, Hildy had inno-
cently opened the wrong upstairs hall window—the
one we leave unscreened. I think Pammy sneaked out
more for a joke, because to our considerable confusion, when we thought she was safely in for the day,
she turned up at the front door.

Pammy was a homing cat; if she'd been alone I
might have let her out; but I couldn't take a chance
on Sherry that late in the day. We sipped our drinks
and admired our cats' curving haunches. I told Hildy
a line I had read somewhere: "They walk thin and sit
fat." We went on talking, probably not about cats. At
some point, they went upstairs.

We were sitting at the far end of the living room,
where we could see the front door. Beyond it a big
police dog appeared with some brownish animal in
its mouth—an animal Siamese-cat size. Our cats were
inside; they had to be inside—the unscreened window
—Hildy made it to the door as fast as I did. The big
police dog looked at us from mild eyes. He put down,
on our stoop, the miniature dachshund he had been
carrying, probably because the dachsie had got tired

of trying to walk so fast. The little light brown dachshund was pretty wet—slobbered on—but seemed refreshed by the lift. The two romped off together.

I said to Hildy, "The way you leaped to the door, you care about the cats as much as I do."

She said, "I was so terrified my heart nearly stopped."

Our cats came down to get dinner. As Pammy went out to the kitchen, I thought her rear end was dragging a bit. She was walking low, and that was so unlike Pammy I watched her carefully. After a few steps she seemed as prancing as ever.

Hildy had teased me about losing my professional standing as a worrier. She had said, "You're slipping badly. You can hardly think of a single thing to worry about any more."

If I had to find something to worry about, I didn't want it to be Pammy. I put the flash of uneasiness out of my mind and thought about our peeling house; we ought to have it painted before another winter.

Hildy thought it shouldn't be repainted the same steel gray. "Let's have a color with more warmth—maybe deeper gray with a dash of cinnamon or burnt sienna. We'll get them to mix some samples."

That was enough to worry about—pleasantly.

IX

Pammy

᠅᠅᠅

THE TERRACE was covered with drop cloths, buckets and ladders, and small boards with samples of paint splashed on as swatches of colors to be examined and debated by humans and cats.

The cats circled and sniffed and did everything but climb ladders. Sherry bolted whenever one of the workmen came near; Pammy made friends and was very helpful each time they shifted their paraphernalia or propped a ladder under another window. The head painter said he liked cats, which was just as well. He was an Italian who spoke very little English, although he spoke much more English than we spoke Italian. He and Hildy exchanged felicitations daily on the way our house was fitting into its new coat. Hildy would say, "Bellissima," and the painter's white teeth and dark eyes would signal delighted agreement.

When it was finished, Hildy and I reclaimed the terrace and sat admiring what we had wrought. We, with the help of Charles Hoffman, the contractor, who had listened to my wife's description of what she wanted and said, "Sort of a moleskin—I think that's the color you're after." He was the contractor who had built the house, and he took a proprietary interest. He said, "Dick, when you asked me to come over and bring color samples, I was afraid you'd married some little dame who wanted a yellow house with silvery gray trim." And all Hildy wanted was moleskin with white; he was very relieved, even enthusiastic. Charles mixed the first samples himself; then sent the head painter, who, he said, had the best eye for mixing colors. Altogether, six humans and two cats had wrought to fine effect.

Pammy seemed to feel responsible for the paint smell that lingered on. She spent two hours washing herself. "Like Lady Macbeth," Hildy said.

Dr. Camuti had once told me that if a cat washed excessively, it might mean she was ill. "It's like trying to get a bad taste out of your mouth."

I thought of that and I went on watching Pammy even more carefully. I have owned a good many cats, and I have read dozens of cat books and written some. So I felt experienced enough to spot any serious symptoms. Several times I thought Pammy's rear end was dragging a bit, but never for more than a few seconds, and I was never quite sure it was dragging at all. It is sometimes a symptom in cats that indicates a progressive kidney or bladder ailment.

But it is rare except among altered males, and then is an indication that the cat is getting old. One cat of mine had died of it but he was eleven at the time, not especially old as cats go, but a good deal older than Pammy, who was only six or seven.

Pammy still went prancing all over the indoors and outdoors. She did suddenly stop jumping up on the counter for her food, and ate from Sherry's pan instead, on the floor. We put her pan on the floor, to humor this newest whim. A day or so later, when I was carving a capon on a kitchen counter, a capon Helen had roasted for us, Pammy jumped to the counter looking for her share. Her leap seemed to be as floating and effortless as ever, which encouraged me. And she went on coming downstairs in that eager bumpety rush, even late at night, to welcome us and roll over at the lady's feet. And leap to the lady's lap whenever Hildy sat down.

Late August steamed in, and Pammy seemed rather listless for two or three days; she didn't eat much, but neither did Sherry.

"I don't like the way she's breathing," Hildy said. "She heaves."

I said, "It's the heat. You'd heave too if you had to wear a fur coat, and could only perspire through your thumbs." But I did go over and listen to Pammy, who was stretched on the cool green tile floor. All I could hear was purring, and there's a theory that as long as a cat is purring, there can't be much the matter. I told Hildy that.

Pammy's eyes were normal; so was her tongue, as far as I could tell. Her fur wasn't spiky. And Sherry didn't avoid her, as a cat will often avoid an ailing companion. The two seemed closer than ever. Several times it occurred to me that Pammy was bringing Sherry more into the family, in the evenings. They would settle together on a table under a lamp, side by side, with their ears crisped whenever Hildy said how beautiful they looked in that pose. They knew it anyway.

Pammy still went outdoors every morning with Sherry, then came back for a brief after-breakfast visit with the lady. When Hildy and I shut ourselves up in our workrooms, Pammy departed again, but two or three times I came down at noon to find her lying on the terrace, shadowed under a chaise. "She isn't running as much," Helen said. We double-checked the cats' toilet pan, which seemed normal. It had to be the heat that had got Pammy down.

I had always had a special love for Pammy. And now that she and the lady adored each other, my feeling was even stronger. Pammy had to be all right. She would be all right as soon as the wind shift came.

And then one afternoon late that same week, I knew Pammy was ill. She began to lie down after a few steps, and when she walked, it was slowly. She had always been a cat who danced.

That evening she did not go to the kitchen for her dinner, although Sherry was there and rattling her pan like a dinner bell. Pammy lay stretched out on the lady's yellow and white slip-covered sofa. Hildy cut tiny pieces of white meat from the refrigerated capon and warmed them in her hands because I had told her that cold food isn't good even for well cats. She took the pan of chicken bits in to Pammy, and Pammy smelled it, then looked up at the lady as if to say, What a nice surprise—I didn't think I was hungry. She ate every last shred of chicken. But then she lay down again and didn't even stretch.

We had a dinner date that night, and I was the one who said we shouldn't break it—that we would take Pammy to the vet's the next morning if she still seemed exhausted.

We did not stay out late. As I turned the car into our driveway, Hildy said, "If she's not at the door to meet us, we'll take her to the vet's right now—even if we have to wake him up."

Pammy did meet us at the door. She rubbed against Hildy's legs and rolled over to have her belly stroked, and she purred. Hildy was wildly relieved. She said, "You were right—it must have been heat prostration." But then she sensed my uneasiness, and said I'd reverted to my old worry habits.

Just the same, she was up and dressed before eight the next morning. And instead of her going downstairs ahead, we went together. Sherry was waiting on the landing—alone.

Pammy lay on the living-room floor. She tried desperately to roll at her lady's feet—and couldn't make it.

Hildy cradled Pammy in her arms while I phoned the vet. Dr. Dann said he had to go out very soon, but he'd wait for us if we hurried. I brought the cat-carrier from the garage, and Hildy grabbed a guest-room towel to line it with. Sherry had finished breakfast and disappeared. When I put Pammy into the carrier, she didn't struggle much. And that was bad, because she had always hated it.

But once the car started moving, she pressed her face against the wire grating and complained with great spirit. The Ridgefield Veterinary Hospital is on the far side of the village, six or seven miles away. I was torn between wanting to drive slowly enough not to jounce our sick cat, and wanting to get her there fast. Hildy kept trying to reassure Pammy, crooning endearments, saying, "You'll feel better soon."

As we went through Ridgefield, Pammy complained louder than ever. Hildy said, "It's not much farther now, darling. We're almost there."

"It's not all that near," I said, as if the three of us were engaged in responsive conversation and I did not want Pammy misled by promises which couldn't be kept.

As soon as Dr. Dann picked Pammy up, she quieted and rested her head against him. He is a very good man with cats, and he handles them well, as not all vets do. He had brought Pammy through a difficult whelping and enteritis, and through virus pneumonia. But that morning he was obviously puzzled. He checked all the things I had checked earlier; her temperature was normal too. He asked me, as a long-time cat owner, what symptoms I had noticed. I mentioned the slowing down. Hildy said, "But first, her breathing was off."

Dr. Dann had put a stethoscope on Pammy's chest earlier. He looked at my wife. "I picked up something in Pammy's lungs that doesn't sound right." He said he would have to keep her there for tests. X rays ought to show what was wrong. He would call us that afternoon.

When Hildy and I walked into the house empty-handed, Sherry was watching from the landing. She turned and raced into our bedroom, wailing on a high, terrible note that tore at our ears and nerves. A dozen times, she raced up and down stairs like a creature crazed by pain, wailing in that haunting way. "But she wasn't even around when we put Pammy in the carrier," Hildy said.

Cats know things that humans will never know.

Sherry wouldn't let either of us come near her. We tried to calm her down even by talking from a distance, but she never stopped keening. After an hour of that I practically pushed her out the front door, thinking if an outing didn't help her, at least it would help us. We already felt upset enough, without that incessant wailing. Sherry was back within five or ten minutes, raced through the entire house again, and then wailed more agonizingly than ever.

When Helen arrived and heard the news, she said, "Pammy is a very determined cat. She never gives up. If she can possibly pull through, she will."

In Sherry's eyes, Hildy and I were somehow responsible for Pammy's terrible absence. Helen was not.

We could hear the murmur of Helen's voice upstairs, going on and on, softly, tenderly, until Sherry finally quieted down for a bit. Helen told us afterward, "Usually when I go in to do your bedroom, Sherry runs away, but this time she wanted to talk. She kept talking to me as if her heart would break."

Dr. Dann phoned to say the X rays didn't show enough. He was doing another set. If the new pictures weren't decisive, he would get a second opinion. Pammy was a very sick cat. It was clear as much from the tone of his voice as from the words he used that he wasn't very hopeful about her.

I tried to prepare Hildy. I even reminded her that Pammy was the one who clawed furniture. I said we could have several pieces upholstered without worrying about their being ripped up. Hildy said, "If Pammy gets well enough to come home, she can rip up any damn thing in the house."

The phone rang around breakfast time the next morning, too early for a friend to call. "You answer it," Hildy said. There was a kind of fading out in her clear, light voice.

And Dr. Dann's voice, on the phone, was very tired. He said, "We've lost Pammy. Five minutes ago." He wanted to do an autopsy to find out why. I said of course.

I hung up and went over to Hildy, and she was crying. So was I. We held on to each other.

In a small way, it helped to have Dr. Dann call us again that same morning, after the autopsy, to say, "It wouldn't have made any difference if you had brought her in earlier." There's a medical term for what Pammy died of, but I have forgotten it. Her chest had filled up with fluids, and nothing could be done. Dr. Dann said, "Pammy didn't have a chance."

Like Helen, like all of us, he knew Pammy would have fought against almost any odds—and won. But she hadn't had a chance.

Neither Hildy nor I felt like working our usual stint at writing that week. I never saw Hildy weed so hard. Whenever she looked up suddenly, looked toward the gap in the stone wall, I knew what she was seeing, wishfully, because I kept seeing that too—our dancing cat coming home.

The place we saw Pammy oftenest—imagined her—was at the foot of the stairs.

Sherry's constant, wailing search made things harder. She couldn't be distracted from grief; the humans wanted to be distracted, and were glad to have the unexpected chore of cleaning out my office.

Hildy, in her survey of our house, had given a long look at my office desk. It was too small for my purposes, or any. I told her a bit wistfully that I had always planned to get, someday, a desk that would have enough room on top for a row of my most-used reference books: Police Department City of New York, *Manual of Police Procedure; Legal Medicine, Pathology and Toxicology*, and a half dozen others. Now they were piled on window sills. And the desk top was so cluttered with loose paper there was no work space; cluttered with notes I might use some time, with letters I might even answer—a debris of unmade decisions.

For my birthday, Hildy had ordered a new desk made, a desk measured to fit the room and accord with my kind of disorder. It had been promised for mid-September. But the day after Pammy died, Hildy told me the desk was being delivered sooner. "To-morrow."

Normally I would have dreaded cleaning out my old desk; now both Hildy and I tackled the job with relief, as another distraction. I shuffled the desk-top papers into a pile; I yanked out overstuffed drawers and gave Hildy the top drawer, which was filled with decisions even longer postponed: with notes for lectures given years before; with road maps of areas I had once thought of driving in; with brochures describing power cultivators I had never bought. I had very little idea what I'd put out of sight and mind, put in the top drawer, whenever the desk top overflowed.

We sat side by side on the office couch, with a wastebasket between us. Did I want to keep this? Hildy would ask me. Was I ever going to answer this letter, I would ask myself. The wastebasket filled up. Then, for a while, Hildy said nothing, and her papers stopped shuffling. She was reading something; she made an odd, choked sound. "Look," she said.

She handed me a typewritten page, and I was embarrassed to see it was verse—my own. In my teens, I had wanted to be a poet. For many who live by words, the desire to write poetry occasionally recurs. It is a desire usually to be resisted. I had had that particular lapse perhaps a dozen years before. And I did not regard it as poetry. I told Hildy that. I said I thought I had thrown it away long ago. I started to crumple it up for the wastebasket, but she said, "No. Because it could be Pammy. Read it." I read, with a strange sense of timelessness; I couldn't even remember which cat, but now I too thought of Pammy:

> Since she is mortal, as am I
> My cat must also some day die.
> But being flame while I am clod
> It will be she will go to God.
>
> Go flickering up the golden flight
> Slit-eyes undazzled by the light
> And pause before the golden chair
> To lick the star-dust from her hair.
>
> Await afraid (yet without fear)
> As goddess once, before her peer.
> —A gentle touch from hand divine
> She'll be God's cat, as she was mine.

"Pammy flickered when she moved," Hildy said. She took the yellowing, half-crumpled sheet of paper and smoothed it out carefully, and put it out of my reach.

Sherry came to the office door and came crying—came, we knew, not to find us, but to find Pammy. For her, there was no finality, as there was for us. Pammy must still be somewhere.

From the day Pammy went to the hospital, Sherry searched and called. When she was eating, she kept breaking off to look up at the counter where Pammy should have been. She would leave a meal half eaten to go seeking again—seeking, calling.

For days she wandered through the house and we left all doors open for her wandering. If a closet door was closed, she attacked it. Pammy had shown her as a kitten how the doors of the house were hung, and whether one clawed to drag them open or pushed against them. Sherry remembered, and looked in every closet a dozen times a day. Pammy had once accidentally shut herself up in the wood closet and yelled to get out. Perhaps Sherry remembered that too; she searched the wood closet oftenest of all.

Every time she came in from outside, she would search the entire house again.

I told Hildy I wondered whether Sherry was searching for a cat, as cat. A cat she had known all her life, and curled with when it was cool for cats, and romped with? The two had been very close. I had always thought Sherry depended on Pammy for whatever assurance she had. But I am wary of putting human feelings in a cat mind. I told Hildy maybe there was merely a sudden, inexplicable emptiness in Sherry's life. She sought, from room to room, something which would fill that emptiness. I said that a human sometimes wakens of mornings with a feeling of desolation, and it may be moments—the moments of coming fully awake—before he remembers why the day to which he has waked seems meaningless. I could remember such wakenings, I told Hildy, from days before we knew each other.

Perhaps, I said, Sherry is living now in some such state of unresolved unhappiness, is wandering and calling out, miserably, through a dim dream of unremembered memories.

Hildy said, "You may evolve all the fancy theories you want. But I know Sherry is looking for Pammy."

I admitted there was a lot in Sherry's behavior to justify that, but I couldn't be certain. Hildy said, "Well, I'm certain."

What was absolutely clear to both of us was that our only cat was miserable. We planned to get another cat, for her sake and ours, but for her sake we wanted to give her time to recover. "We must make her know first she will always be our number-one cat," Hildy said. "It's like having a new baby. First you have to make the older child feel more loved and secure than ever."

Sherry was making it difficult for Hildy to love her—difficult even to get near her. If I approached her alone, I could stroke her a few minutes before she struggled free to go on with her search. After a week or so, the frenzy of the search diminished a little, we

supposed as her hope faded. She would sit in a room
with us again, at a distance, and doze under a lamp.
But then, for no reason we could see, hope would
come back; she would leap up again and go to look
for Pammy—or look for an end to the ache of unde-
fined sorrow.

She began to come over and stand in front of us
and look up as if asking us to tell her what had happened. There was a note in her voice I had never
heard before.

She had forgiven me enough so that she would
sit on my lap, as Pammy had done, when we listened
together for the lady's footsteps. But with Sherry, the
quick steps were a signal of danger. As soon as she
heard Hildy on the stairs she would leap off my lap
and run.

She leaped off as usual one late afternoon. Hildy
walked across the long room and came to sit beside
me. Sherry slunk out from under a table and began
her usual cautious, furtive detour, preferably under
cover, to get to the kitchen. Hildy spoke to her, as she
often did—with affection.

Sherry halted. She walked over, very slowly, to
the sofa we sat on, and looked up at the lady.

I could see her tense her muscles; her long, lean
body stiffened over the crouching legs. Then she
walked away, even more slowly.

She came back—tensed her muscles again. And

suddenly she was on the lady's lap and settling in as if she'd rehearsed it for months.

Hildy sat absolutely still. She murmured, "I'm almost afraid to breathe. What should I do? Is it all right if I put my hand on her back?"

"Stroke her," I said. "Don't give her time to change her mind."

It may have been three or four minutes later when Hildy said, "Now I know what you meant about her purr. I never heard a cat throb so hard."

X

Sherry

THERE WAS NOTHING gradual about it. From then on, she threw herself into our lives, and into our laps. There was never so much cat. There was never purring so loud and constant.

There was no distinction made between Hildy and me. She was as utterly the lady's cat as she was mine. As we sat side by side, she would, instantly, jump to the sofa with us. She would sit on Hildy's lap; she would move to mine; she would return to Hildy's, lap-hopping. She would stretch on the sofa, usually on Hildy's side of it, and speak up loudly, demanding caress, and respond in a rolling ecstasy. We got out the long-handled scrub brush and took turns brushing her; when one of us got brusher's cramp, the other took over, while Sherry rippled with pleasure, and vibrated with purring.

She no longer sought Pammy. Her transference was total.

It was touching to us both, and we were, of course, pleased. We were also a little overwhelmed, mentally as well as physically. Even people who are very fond of cats, as I had long been, and Hildy had become, like to sit down sometimes without a cat. We would have preferred a little time free to pay attention to each other. It would have been pleasant to lift a drink without the virtual certainty that a cat would jostle it half empty between table and lips. Sherry wanted at least one of our four hands free every moment, to stroke her.

We didn't tell her that was a bit overdoing it. We told her she was a beautiful cat, our one and only cat, that she would be Number One Cat forever.

And now that we had only one cat to look at, we were struck even more by her beauty. "That lovely creamy white front," Hildy would say. "And her eyes are much bigger than most cats'." After a brushing: "Look how sleek she is. Remember the night she sat across the room and watched while we brushed Pammy—sat like a stone image, watching? I can hardly bear to think of how she must have felt then."

It seemed to both of us that we had not done justice to the Sherry cat.

Perhaps that was sentimental of us, since it was Sherry who had not done justice to us; she who had chosen to be a disturbed onlooker, a secondary cat. But sentimentality is merely sentiment misplaced, and I don't think our feeling for Sherry was that. We understood now that she had been starved for love, and too proud, too afraid, to show it. We tried very hard, and with growing love, to make it up to her.

But it was a relief, after two or three weeks, when our insatiably loving cat moderated her demands. Perhaps a sense of feline dignity reasserted itself in a cat who, after years, for the first time had learned devotion to humans. After all, she may have thought to herself, you are a cat. It is unbecoming for a cat to behave as a subservient dog behaves.

She did not withdraw in any real sense. She was in the room with us often. In the evenings, instead of retiring upstairs, she would usually lie on another sofa, companionably near, or on the chair by the fire.

Hildy had enjoyed a column in the weekly Ridgefield *Press* called, first, "Spring Pips," then "Summer Larks." Now as I began to build fires again in short cool dusks, we debated what the column might be christened next. I thought perhaps "Autumn Falls." But it simply vanished altogether, so that Hildy could no longer read me tidbits from that—only from the police log. She liked Officer Rotunda—the fine rolling sound of him—and would even follow his performance of duty on a traffic misdemeanor. Sherry never tried to bash through a newspaper as Pammy had done: she would simply lie down on it every chance she got. I never gave her a chance. I always read the *Times* held up in mid-air, as any sensible man reads a paper. Hildy would spread it open, flat,

on the sofa beside her, and turn pages as she read.
Sherry grew adept at stretching full length on a page
to cover as much as possible. Then Hildy would
stroke our cat and try to read around the edges of her.
Once she said, "Listen to this: 'LOST: six-month-old
Siamese cat, male, answers to name of Booful. Wearing aquamarine blue rhinestone collar. Reward.'"
We agreed that the Siamese male had undoubtedly
slipped his collar and taken it on the lam to escape
from a rhinestone existence.

Sherry, whenever we mentioned the word *cat*,
would listen intensely, eyes half closed, ears up. We
discovered by late fall that she would listen just
as attentively to poetry—some of it. Whenever I read
aloud to Hildy, Sherry sat boat fashion, head held at
attention, till I picked something that displeased her
—Eliot's "Macavity" for one, and Ogden Nash's "Song
to Pier Something or Other." Then she would bury
her head in the cushion and put her paws over her
ears. She behaved in the same rude fashion toward
Ella Fitzgerald singing certain Irving Berlin songs.
As far as we could tell, her favorite record was
Rodgers and Hammerstein's *Carousel;* we were rather
exasperated that she picked that over *Oklahoma!* or
The King and I or *My Fair Lady*.

Even when our musical selection or our choice of
an old movie on the late show was not to her taste,
she seldom left the room. She was too happy being
with us.

Hildy likes to wear long things at home in the evening, and she was trying now to slant her choice to Sherry: no dark velveteens that collected cat hairs in layers, or the Persiany embroidered shift that caught even well-behaved claws. Those could be saved for New York. She got out a large fuzzy yellow mohair stole and Helen made it into an evening skirt. (This was Helen's idea; she sews as well as she does everything else.) It turned out to be a smashing success, and Hildy said happily, "Now I can shed on Sherry."

But the skirt terrified Sherry. When she landed on the sofa beyond Hildy and was ready for lap-sitting, she would look with reproach at the mohair skirt and, if there was room between us for a landing, jump clear over Hildy and sit on me, although the lady was always better sitting. If there wasn't room for a clean leap, she would screw up her courage and walk across the skirt, stepping lightly as a cat can and as briefly as possible. We never quite figured it out. Perhaps Sherry did think the skirt would shed on her. Or that the lady had no business wearing the hair of a stupid goat.

Her behavior the night of the Great Blackout was unexpected too. Most of the Eastern Seaboard went dark, but with radio and television dead, we hadn't realized the extent of the power failure. I told Hildy, speaking from considerable experience, that this was a local failure—probably just a Lewisboro blackout. Like all country dwellers, I always have extra candles on hand, and I put them all around the living room—on the bar, on coffee tables and lamp tables. We had always had candles burning on the dining-room table at dinner; Sherry had never paid any attention to them. They were off limits, anyway, when humans were eating.

That night of the blackout, Sherry sat and looked at the candle burning on the coffee table in front of Hildy and me. After staring at it reflectively for a minute, her eyes red in its soft light, she jumped to the table and, with great caution, approached the flame. She put her nose almost against it, sniffing. She withdrew with a start, but she didn't say anything, so it was evident that she hadn't singed her whiskers or her nose.

She looked around the room and saw other candles, and she went to each candle—on the bar, on the other tables—and sniffed at each. It was as if candles had been kept from her all her life; her tour was a voyage of exploration, of discovery. We watched her face lit by candles and thought how our fearful cat had changed.

She went out every morning after breakfast, but her outings were much briefer. At frequent intervals she would appear outside a door and call to be let in. We thought she came for reassurance, wanting to make certain we were still around. Sometimes we were shut away in our workrooms and she would complain bitterly to Helen about our closed-door policy toward cats. We explained to Sherry that she ought to be glad we were back at work. A supply of junior beef, we told her, depended on the clatter of typewriter keys and the shuffle of pencil on paper fixed to a clipboard. Sherry didn't seem particularly convinced. She wanted company.

We had already begun looking for another cat. We had called two cat breeders recommended by Dr. Dann, but neither had a Siamese cat the right age. The right age, I thought, might be perhaps eight months to a year old. Not a kitten—I was fairly sure of that. A kitten, I thought, probably would terrify Sherry, and in her terror she might well kill it. She is a long cat, large for her breed and sex. Siamese queens are usually small cats. Sherry is deceptively powerful; a kitten would stand no chance with her, and her probable reaction was unpredictable, at least by me. She might, of course, even run from it.

And any cat, however mature, would take some getting used to. We couldn't merely buy a youngish female, have her spayed, and throw her casually in with Sherry. It might be tantamount to throwing her into a lion's den. I told Hildy I suspected Sherry, basically, was not at all fond of cats (except Pammy). "She may have a touch of ailurophobia," I said. This is not especially unusual; Martini had detested cats. She had not cared much for dogs, either.

I thought if we widened our search we could probably find a cat who seemed suitable to us. But to Sherry?

The idea of bringing home a new cat right then began to seem more and more impractical. We would have to be there to introduce the newcomer and Sherry, and supervise the adjusting, and maybe act as buffer. It might take months. That would mean we'd have to stay on through the winter. We had planned to move into the New York apartment in November, then go on to Key West for February and March. I was determined to get Hildy away from the raw weather, and make sure that she'd have a healthy winter for a change. I said we'd have to wait till spring to get a new cat. But that still left the problem of Sherry.

In past winters, Helen and her husband had stayed in the house while I was away, to look after it and cats. That was no longer possible. Helen would still come in every day, but one cat couldn't stay alone at night. Especially not Sherry. And we couldn't board her at a vet's. When Sherry had been spayed, Dr. Dann had called and asked me to take her home early, although normally he preferred a longer convalescence under observation. But there was nothing much he could do, he said, for a cat who had decided to starve herself to death. Sherry's grim experience of being shut up as a kitten made tight confinement at a vet's out of the question.

To take her into New York with us, and on to Key West, wouldn't be a solution for her or us. Sherry was a country cat; she had never traveled. The apartment on Ninth Street is small even for the two of us; the place in Key West even smaller. And a trip south would mean days of Sherry shut up in a carrier.

"We're responsible for her," Hildy said. "We'll have to stay here with her if we can't work something out."

I said our own happiness came before a cat's. But we kept postponing our going, while we debated our cat's future.

It was Helen who solved the problem of Sherry's winter and our own. She offered to take Sherry to live with her over the winter in her apartment in Ridgefield. "That is, if you think it's a good idea," she said.

Hildy and I thought it was merely ideal. For all of Sherry's life, Helen had been one of the few humans she trusted. Helen's apartment was warm and comfortable and roomy. Sherry could not go out hunting in Ridgefield, but during the winter she and Pammy had been inclined to stay indoors anyway.

Two days before we were to drive a loaded car into New York, I got the carrier out of the garage and put it on the floor to warm up. This time, I made very sure Sherry didn't see it till I'd got a good grip on her. With the help of Helen and Hildy, I managed to get our cat inside and shut the lid. Then I washed the blood off my hands. We drove to Helen's, Sherry screeching her head off the whole way.

When we went inside, we were careful to close all doors before we opened the carrier. Sherry crouched motionless for a minute or two. Then she leaped out and ran for the nearest cover, a small table, about the right size for a cat to crouch under. She crouched and glared at us. Hildy and I said all the fatuous, unhelpful things one says at such times to cats. Sherry was too angry, too terrified, even to snarl in answer.

Hildy and I drove home to a house without a cat. By late afternoon, we were asking each other every half hour if we ought to call up and ask how our cat was making out. Hildy said, "We act like parents who've sent their child off to boarding school for the first time." And I said, Yes, we must be more sensible about this; we must give Sherry time to adjust—twenty-four hours at least.

The house seemed incredibly empty. The next morning, somehow Hildy and I both managed to be in the kitchen when Helen arrived. We tried, with no special success, to make our questions sound not too anxious.

Sherry had finally come out from under the

table. She had found a closet and spent the night hidden there. No, she had not eaten. No, she had not used her toilet pan. I told Hildy that was normal, that Sherry was acting like any cat in a strange place.

We went to New York the next day. Sherry had come out of the closet. She had eaten. "And I let her sleep in my bed with me," Helen said, "to make her feel more secure."

"Do you think," Hildy asked me, "that Sherry will expect to sleep with us when she comes home?"

I said I didn't know what Sherry would expect. But I knew one thing she wasn't going to get.

For Christmas, Hildy gave me a new wheelbarrow. And Helen reported that Sherry had played for hours Christmas Day with a crocheted mouse. We were glad to hear our cat was happy. But we felt a little wistful that it didn't sound as if she were missing us much.

XI

Lady Without a Cat

🐾🐾🐾

THE FIRST REPORT we had in Key West on Sherry was that she now "liked everybody." Guests came to the apartment and as soon as they made laps, Sherry went to sit on them. "Even if they don't especially like cats," Helen wrote, "Sherry is all over them."

We thought that was going too far.

Sherry was sleeping very well—in Helen's bed: "She doesn't wake me till just about time for my alarm to go off. And I'm glad to have her for warmth these cold nights."

Hildy and I were hunched over an electric heater as we read this. The night we arrived in Key West the temperature thudded down to 50 degrees and a northeast wind blew. Our little rented apartment was right on the Atlantic; it was rather like living on a small wooden ship in a February gale.

Tourists, determined that the subtropics be subtropical, went shivering in shorts. Hildy and I wore sweaters and dug out extra blankets.

It warmed up in four or five days, as it always

does in the island city. We sat on the balcony over the ocean and covered ourselves with oily gook and watched the pelicans. We thought Sherry wouldn't have quite believed in pelicans; I don't myself. Shrimp boats went by in coveys, their masts draped in a rainbow of nets. Each morning submarines went out and destroyers followed them, beginning the game of hare and hounds which the Navy plays from the Key West base.

Hildy's hacky cold evaporated in the sun. Her sinus was nonexistent; she said she'd never had such an incredibly healthy winter. She had never before eaten stone crabs or pompano or yellowtail, all Key West specialties. We made up for her lost time in seafood restaurants. But we went quite often to an Italian restaurant that had almost no seafood; we went for the cats. A half dozen cats, mostly strays, would swirl around customers' tables, a fickle crew that went where the pickings were best. We fed them shamelessly, so that they would stick around our table longer.

When we were driving around in our rented car, Hildy would say, "Stop! Oh, Dick, stop. I saw a yellowish brown cat go over that hedge and it may be a Siamese."

It was never a Siamese. But we were ready to like almost any kind of cat—even long-hairs. Hildy asked me if Sherry would mind another breed when we got a new cat in the spring. I said cats had no prejudices whatever; we might consider a Burmese, or a striped tabby. Somehow we always wound up talking about another Siamese.

There were times, reading Helen's reports, when we wondered if we'd even get back our own Siamese. Sherry sounded entirely too contented where she was. Even her need to hunt had, unexpectedly, been satisfied. She could not, in the village of Ridgefield go out and look for game. Obligingly, game had come to her. For the first time since Helen had lived in the apartment, mice had started to come into it, which was very ill-advised of the mice. Sherry was catching them with relish. In all respects, she seemed to be having a wonderful time, and not at all wishing we were there.

"Will she ever want to come back?" Hildy said. "Will she remember us when she sees us?"

XII

The Resolute Tail

ᘒᘒᘒ

WE OPENED the carrier in our living room; Sherry crouched and glared. Either she didn't remember Hildy and me, or she remembered us all too well as betrayers, deserters. She leaped out of the carrier and skidded wildly on a tile floor she didn't remember, either. She went whizzing, skidding, in a dizzy round of the whole downstairs, then took cover under a bed in the guest room. Helen, Hildy and I crooned and coaxed, and got only more snarls and glares. Even Helen was a betrayer now, because she had delivered Sherry into our hands.

"We'll have to let her alone for a day or two," I told my anxious wife. "She can't be rushed. Don't worry about her." I cited case after case in my experience of cats who had taken their own proud pace in coming around after an absence.

By midafternoon, I, the non-worrying cat expert, was lying on the floor beside the guest-room bed, urging Sherry to trust us. Hildy came in and found me, and said comforting things to the cat and its

prostrate owner. When I went off to unpack, Hildy
took the next shift on the guest-room floor. Sherry
had stopped snarling and was crying in a desolate
way that unnerved us more. But she wouldn't come
out. Finally Hildy and I staggered up, blearily, to
take a much-needed catnap.

Later we listened to the news; we had a drink.
And Sherry crept out of hiding long enough to eat
her dinner. Around nine or ten o'clock, she came as
far as the living room and glanced up at the light
glinting out through the shutters of the liquor cup-
board. For some reason, she had always checked on
that light every time she walked by it. Perhaps she
liked the striping of shadows it threw. Right after
Pammy died, we had even kept on the light in the
daytime, hoping it might comfort our small wandering cat.

"She remembers," I said to Hildy. "She knows
she's come home."

The next day, she settled down in our laps and
lives again.

We were surprised and thankful that she remembered her old pattern so well she never made the
slightest attempt to stay in our bedroom all night.
But in the mornings, the minute Hildy or I gave a
first waking stir in bed, Sherry would start talking
outside our door: it was time for slug-a-beds to get up
and feed a starving cat.

Hildy often called through the door to give Sherry a countdown: "Now I'm putting on my robe. . . . Now allow ten seconds for lipstick, or ten and a half. . . ." Silence while Sherry counted. "Now I'm combing my hair. . . ." Impatient screech here. "But my hair is a mess. You wouldn't want me to appear unkempt at breakfast, would you?"

Sherry indicated, in strong language, that she preferred an unkempt sort to the sort who starved cats.

After her own breakfast, she would wait long enough to greet me and make sure her family was all of a piece before she went out. As April warmed into May, Sherry stayed out longer and longer. She lost the rather sagging belly she had acquired in the winter months indoors. She was sleek and taut, and newly assured. "If only her tail wouldn't droop," Hildy said occasionally. We couldn't help remembering Pammy's high, resolute tail.

We went on talking about when and where we would get another cat. Every time Helen heard us, her handsome face would set the way it does when she's dubious or disapproving. "Sherry is so happy being the one and only," she said. "She's come out of herself. She's like a new cat, now that she's the center of attention."

I had always believed that two cats are better than one—the principle of diversifying, of humans not putting all their affection in one basket. I had been looking forward to another cat as much for our own enjoyment as for Sherry's. But Hildy and I knew that *we* didn't need a second cat to be happy. And if it wouldn't make Sherry happy—might even throw her backward—then what was the point? We decided that as long as we had Sherry, she must be our one and only cat. She had lived too long under another cat's paw.

In late May, on our first anniversary, Hildy and I went to the inn where we'd gone on our wedding day to listen to Peter Walters play Gershwin. We came home late; while I was getting out my key, I saw Hildy peer in through the glass, and I knew she was thinking of how Pammy had always rushed down bumpety-bumpety to welcome us.

Sherry never came to the door to greet us; if she happened to be on a sofa, she stayed there; if she was snoozing on an upstairs bed, she stayed there. Sometimes after five or ten minutes she would saunter down, with an air of, Oh, well, now that you're back, I don't mind if you stroke me. The night of our first anniversary, she did eventually join us for a nightcap.

As an anniversary present, Hildy asked to go to Pinchbeck's greenhouse again. This time she picked out impatiens plants because they are alleged to thrive in shade, and we have plenty of that—too much —by the terrace. She got red and white geraniums too, to line up across the front of our moleskin-gray house. And alyssum for ground cover. All very practical—she even asked the price of each plant. All very different from the lady's first visit to Pinchbeck's.

But, when she's dressing after a shower, she still sings things like "I've Got My Love To Keep Me Warm." Sherry sits with me then, or on me, and we both listen to the singing and the quick footsteps. One day Hildy came down late, and I said, "Sherry was worried. She didn't hear you singing and she wanted to know why. She wants to know if you're upset about anything." Sometimes it is convenient to utilize a cat's curiosity.

Hildy looked puzzled. She said, "I wonder why I wasn't singing—I guess because I was running late and I hurried. Tell Sherry that was the only reason. I've never been so happy in my life. I get happier all the time."

Sherry said yah-*ow;* she may have been saying the same thing as the lady.

A week or so afterward, I got out my key late in the evening, to let us in, and my wife gave that brief, wishful look through the glass, then suddenly pounded on the door with her fists—rather small fists —calling, "Sherry, come down. . . . Sherry, come down this minute and welcome us."

I knew why she did it—she needed to make

sounds to keep from being sentimental about a dead cat.

I turned the key and we walked in. "Look," I said.

Sherry was rushing down the stairs, not bumpety as Pammy had done, but rushing, to the lady who had called her.

Since then, Sherry comes to us almost every time she is called—something I have never seen a cat do before. Of course, this doesn't always hold true when she is out hunting on a summer day.

She stops in for lunch, and a brief nap and lap-sit. We let her go out again afterward, because now we know she'll always come home to her family.

When she rushed in once panting like a dog, after a strenuous morning's work, Hildy said, "Where did you go?—what did you catch?—don't tell me. I'd rather not know."

I had just cut asparagus one noon, and was washing it at the faucet in back of the house, when I heard something scream. And scream . . . and scream.

Sherry came trotting through the gap from the meadow with a small rabbit in her mouth. She put it down on the lawn and looked at me for approval, before she pounced again. Helen had seen her through the kitchen window and ran out. While Sherry was repeating this game of cat-and-catch, Helen and I managed to run interference—for the rabbit. We blocked Sherry off from her prey till the baby rabbit recovered enough speed to escape over the wall. We dragooned a furious Sherry inside. Helen said, "It's a good thing Mrs. Lockridge wasn't down yet, to hear that poor screaming little rabbit."

Sherry was bristling mad at both Helen and me; she wouldn't touch her lunch. She made it clear she still planned to have lunch out. She raised such hell I had to let her out, after I figured the rabbit had a ten-minute start and could have gone to ground.

Sherry went over the wall at the exact spot the rabbit had vanished. Helen and I congratulated each other on having at least foiled her plan to picnic on the lawn.

Hildy emerged from her workroom and I couldn't resist telling her what had happened. As long as the story had a happy ending, I thought she'd enjoy it. She did; but she said, "It's the first time Sherry brought anything home. I almost wish I'd been here to see it."

We stretched out on two chaises under the ash tree, for a pre-lunch drink. We exchanged our usual vague, courteous questions about how work had gone that morning. The answers on my side are apt to vary from, "All right, I guess," to, "Terrible. . . . The reader is going to know who the murderer is long before Heimrich does." I have no notion what either of us said that day, in our progress-nonprogress reports. We were talking mostly about Sherry. I told Hildy I felt rather mean about cheating Sherry out of her rabbit. I don't really care that much about baby rabbits—they grow up to be big. I thought again how Sherry had rushed home in triumph, to show us, and I felt even meaner. "She'll never do that again," I said. "From now on, she'll know enough not to trust us."

It seemed shabby treatment for a cat that had finally, after so many years, learned to love and trust humans totally—well, almost totally . . . no cat is that gullible. "This is one day she won't even come home before dark," I said. "She may stay out all night."

Hildy said we could hardly blame Sherry for reacting that way.

"She's coming around the front," Helen yelled, from an upstairs window. "With something in her mouth again."

This time, Sherry trotted right past the terrace— on parade with her prey. "It's a bird," Hildy said. "It's not a rabbit—it's a bird."

It was quite a large starling; Sherry halted long enough to make sure we saw it. She even circled around to Hildy's side, to be doubly sure the lady had a good look. The instant we got up and went toward her, she hurried off with her squeaking, flapping catch—but only twenty or thirty feet across the lawn. She dropped the bird under a maple tree and began the cruel game all cats play—torture before the kill. It was impossible to get near enough for a rescue operation. Each time we tried, Sherry simply removed herself and the dying bird—out of reach but always in our sight. To interfere would only prolong the torture. We had to give up. Hildy tried to be calm, but she kept covering her eyes, and quivering. I said, "You have to remember she's a cat."

"I've been telling myself we have hundreds of starlings," Hildy said. "And only one cat. And I keep saying to myself, Birdbrain, birdbrain—I hope they can't feel pain any more than fish." But she was so shaken that as soon as I knew the bird was dead— Sherry started munching—I made a final rush. Sherry got away all right, leaping over a wall, but in such a hurry she forgot to take her catch. I disposed of it fast. When she came back, she searched all over the side of the lawn. A large woodchuck came from the meadow and ambled past. Sherry paused in her search to look at it thoughtfully.

Hildy moaned, "Oh, no! It's so big—she mustn't try—she'd get killed."

I assured my frantic wife that Sherry had only an academic interest; cats are too bright to tilt at woodchucks.

The woodchuck went back where it had come from. Sherry went on looking for her dead bird. We urged her to give up and come in. "You've proved your point," Hildy called. "I wish you hadn't picked on a bird, but all is forgiven—come home."

Sherry ignored our pleas. When Helen called us to lunch, our cat was still looking for her lost trophy.

She wasn't there when we went out again a half hour later. We debated whether to weed the zinnias or thin the alyssum. But it was such a hot day we stalled; we sat on our tree-shaded terrace and told each other that chores put off till tomorrow are all the better for it.

Helen called from the kitchen. "She's coming . . . she's coming . . . she. . . ." Her voice cracked, like an excited radio announcer's. "Believe it or not, she has *something in her mouth!*"

Having been announced, Sherry entered, audience front. She had a plump brown object in her mouth—tail dangling—squeaking—but I wasn't sure what it was till she dropped it on the grass at the edge of the flagstones. "A mouse," I said. "A pretty good-sized mouse, too."

The fat brown creature ran along the grass right toward us; Hildy shrank back, and I remembered how she is about mice. I started to tell her to go inside, when she got up, walked right to the edge, and said, "Sherry, you're a great, great hunter. We're very proud of you, darling."

Sherry nodded, acknowledging this belated tribute, before she went back to the game of pounce. I think perhaps it was more than a game that day. It was an exhibition. Sherry let the mouse run around and around the terrace, and Hildy said, "This is good for both of us. It's time I got over my foolishness." She stood bravely, lovingly, calling out praises to our cat. Even exhortations. Fifteen or twenty minutes later, Sherry settled down, in our sight, to eat the mouse. Hildy said, "I think we should let her enjoy this one to the end." Sherry did; she kept looking over at us. I can't truthfully say my wife was looking at Sherry during that final phase of the hunt, but she was still very proud. She had me assure her over and over that no other cat of my acquaintance had ever bagged three catches in two hours. "We should have had witnesses," Hildy said, "and had it vouched for or notarized or something—like marlin." But she kept her head turned away from the lunch party.

Sherry finished, and strolled across the lawn. I said to Hildy, "Look—look at her tail."

We stood arm and arm and watched our cat coming home with her tail held high.